Daughter of the Cherokee Strip

Philip Wayman

Printed in Victoria, Canada

National Library of Canada Cataloguing in Publication Data

Wayman, Phil, 1922-
    Daughter of the Cherokee Strip / Phil Wayman.
ISBN 1-4120-0431-4
    1. Wayman, Mildred Secord. 2. Frontier and pioneer
life—Oklahoma. 3. Teachers—Oklahoma—Biography. 4. Oklahoma—Biography. I. Title.
LA2317.L26A3 2003   976.6'05'092
                 C2003-902986-7

TRAFFORD

This book was published *on-demand* in cooperation with Trafford Publishing.
On-demand publishing is a unique process and service of making a book available for retail sale to the public taking advantage of on-demand manufacturing and Internet marketing. **On-demand publishing** includes promotions, retail sales, manufacturing, order fulfilment, accounting and collecting royalties on behalf of the author.

Suite 6E, 2333 Government St., Victoria, B.C. V8T 4P4, CANADA
Phone   250-383-6864   Toll-free   1-888-232-4444 (Canada & US)
Fax   250-383-6804   E-mail   sales@trafford.com
Web site   www.trafford.com   TRAFFORD PUBLISHING IS A DIVISION OF TRAFFORD
HOLDINGS LTD.
Trafford Catalogue #03-0800   www.trafford.com/robots/03-0800.html

10   9   8   7   6   5   4   3

PREFACE

It was not the Gold Seekers or fur trappers who conquered the west. It was not the migrant tribes of people who moved from place to place. Colorful cowboys herded cattle across the best of the grassland but did not subdue it. It was the farmer with a family who fenced the field, built a home and put down deep roots in the soil that transformed the American heartland into the nations bread basket.

The largest land rush of American history occurred in 1893. It was into the land of the Chisholm Trail and the buffalo hunting grounds of the Cherokee Indian nation.

This is the true story of a pioneer family that fulfilled what the Psalmist said: *As arrows in the hand of a mighty man, so are children of the youth: Happy is the man who has his quiver full of them. They shall not be ashamed but they shall speak with the enemies in the gate.**

A family's true story of living through the three great social and economic upheavals of twentieth century; The Depression, Dust Bowl days, and World War II.

Enjoy with us what gave us Joy. Laugh with us, or cry if you want to. Know that you are laughing and crying with real people who loved much and cared a whole lot.. *Ps. 127:4,5

Table of Contents

History Of The Cherokee Strip

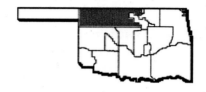

The Cherokee Strip was the Northwest part of the Indian Territory which later became the state of Oklahoma. The US Government established the territory in 1828 as a place to move Indian tribes from southeastern United States. In history it was called the TRAIL OF TEARS. The land strip between the Red river and the border of Kansas was a part of the Louisiana Purchase bought by Thomas Jefferson from France in 1804.

The Cherokee tribe was given a strip of land in Northwest Indian Territory for hunting buffalo. The land strip was 50 miles wide and 200 miles long adjacent to the Kansas southern border. Following the Civil War the US Government acted against the Cherokee nation because they had given loyalties to the confederacy.

At that time the Indian nations were paid .47 per acre to allow the Osages, Kaws, Pawnees, Nez Perce, Ponca, and Tonkawa tribes to be settled on the eastern part of Indian territory. The notable Nez Perce Chief Joseph was brought to Indian Territory after his attempted escape to Canada. However Chief

Joseph was finally moved to Nespelem, Washington where his grave is visited to this day.

In the 1870's the expanding railroads had reached as far west as Dodge City, Kansas. The Texas ranchers needed to reach the railhead to ship huge herds of longhorn cattle to eastern markets. The fertile grazing lands of Indian Territory lay between thousands of head of cattle and the railheads at Abilene or Dodge City, Kansas. Jesse Chisholm, a half Cherokee, found a route through Oklahoma where cattle could be driven slowly all summer and fattened on the buffalo grass of the Cherokee strip.

Since the grazing lands were a part of the Cherokee nation, the drivers paid a tribute of forty cents per head for use of the land. In 1883 the Cherokee Strip Cattlemen Association leased all the land for $100,000 per year until 1890. The Chisholm trail was not a head to tail trail but a wide grazing swath taken slowly so that cattle gained weight while traveling from one watering hole to another . The trail followed the general vicinity of what is now US 81. South of Enid it divided with the western trail going to Dodge City and the eastern trail to Abilene.

Many Cowboy songs and stories came from the five months ride up the Chisholm trail. A good cowboy earned $30. a month and beans, If he had a horse to ride. Many disputes arose over right-of-ways and who owned what. This led to petition for the US government to buy the Cherokee Strip for settlement.

In 1884, David Payne put 1500 settlers in central Oklahoma. These People were called Sooners because they chose their claim before it was staked. They hid out until opening day whereupon they were already there when that part was opened for settlement in 1889.

The Cherokee nation struck a deal with the US government to sell seven million Acres of the Cherokee strip for $1.40 per Acre. Government crews platted the area into 160 Acre tracts with each square mile surrounded with an access road. When this was done the opening date of the largest land grab in US History was set for Sept 16, 1893. Forty thousand homesteads were made available to the first one who placed a flag on his choice tract of land.

An estimated 75,000 settlers gathered on the southern border of Kansas. They were from many states and immigrants from European countries. It was a warm sunny day and a dense pall of dust hung along the starting line.

There were horse drawn buggies, wagons loaded with possessions, prairie schooner with families, men and women on foot or horseback: The sun bore down on impatient throngs waiting for the sound of the noon gun. To be first on choice land demanded the fastest way to get there before dark.

James Monroe Secord taught school at Argonia, Kansas. He was my Grandfather. He was a descendent on his mother's side of the scotch MORE clan who settled in Roxbury, New York a century and a half earlier. The Secord name came from the Sicaurds who were Canadian emigrants. They had fled the Huegenot persecution in France.

James was forty-two years old with a young wife Cora (Surface) just twenty five. They had a two year old boy (Arthur) and a daughter (Mildred) six months old. James had a fast mule hitched to a buggy with a barrel of water and his lunch. The plan was to drive straight south twenty five miles to the flat land beyond the Salt Fork of the Arkansas River. Cora, with her eighteen-year-old brother, John, was to come more slowly with the children and a wagon load of supplies needed for a homestead. The wagon was pulled by a team of mules named Jack and Maud.

The Race For The Land

"BANG!" The guns announced the time. James set out with his fast mule. Cora waited until the dust settled and started out more slowly with her family in the covered Wagon. Some who were on foot stepped over the line and planted their flag on first available plot that others passed over in their hurry. With fifty miles of possibilities, the grass looked greener just ahead.

The day had it humor and its hardships. In One case, we do not know whether to laugh or cry. An Immigrant family came to the starting line with a team of spirited horses hitched to a wagon that was piled high with all their possessions. The man was in the drivers seat with the reins in his hands and the woman was perched high on top of the furniture. A bed mattress made a comfortable as possible ride for her. The piece was not secured well. When the Gun sounded the startled horses bolted ahead so fast that the mattress and the lady wound up amid the dust and confusion of those left behind.

The man did not look back and could not hear above the din and excitement of the moment, the anguished screams from his wife. He left her and mattress laying in the dust as the wagon disappeared in the distance. Nobody knows the end of that story. If the man discovered his wife's plight too late to return for her, he would jeopardize a best choice in the land grab. I hope he did not feel that it would be better to get another wife later on rather than return to face the ire of the one he had. Those were intense days and men did stupid things under pressure.

James Secord got along pretty well traveling lightly. He found a crossing of the Salt Fork and arrived at a plot twenty-five miles inland by night fall. Both he and the mule were worn out. He planted his flag, lit his kerosene lantern, and guarded his claim all night against possible claim jumpers.

Cora did not fare so well. She had her twenty year old brother, John, to drive the team while she cared for her two small children. She prepared sandwiches from sardines for the noon time. Some sardines were left in the can. Night fell in the middle of nowhere. She built a fire and by lantern light fed the family some food. Her brother, John, found the sardine can with the unused portion. He decided to make an easy meal of them. In the night he got dreadfully sick.

Cora spent a fearful night with nowhere to turn for help. John was in severe pain. The children were fretful and cross. The Coyotes howling and the mournful hoot of owls made her spend a fearful, sleepless night on the prairie.

By morning John was better. They resumed their journey. How she was able to find the right place is a miracle. Every prairie homestead looks alike. By the second evening before dark James spied the wagon load of family & possessions in the distance. They had a joyous reunion. Being devout people they thanked God and took courage.

They pitched their tent and began the long process of making a home on the prairies. It was fall of the year and too late to prepare for crops.. James took his family back to teach the school year starting in October. He returned in March the next year to open some sod. The stubborn prairie responded reluctantly to the plow. It was hard work to break up the ground that had been matted for milleniums with buffalo grass. He planted a garden and some kaffir corn for a crop.

James and Cora lived in a tent with the two children while a clapboard house was built. Coldwater creek was right across the road to the east of the property, but water did not flow all year.

The big disappointment with the place was that a dug well only produced bitter water. They had to haul in water from a distance. The first two years were very dry and the crops were small. With a couple of cows and a garden he managed to feed his family. the Kaffir corn was ground up for porridge and also popped like popcorn. They discovered that winter wheat could do well in the Cherokee Strip. This furnished winter grazing for cattle and a cash crop the following summer.

James was convinced of need for school and church in the community. He helped organize and build the Star country school that doubled on Sunday for a church. His efforts were always spent for welfare of his family. The fields finally began to respond to wheat and the family expanded to ten children.

A big two story house was built with six bedrooms. A cistern was dug to catch the rain water from the roof. This was adequate for the family needs all the year. Rain water without minerals in it caused physical problems later that shortened Cora's life at sixty-three

James was much older but outlived his wife several years. He was a devout Christian who made a strong impact in the community where he lived. The strong discipline of life in the Cherokee Strip helped all ten of the children of James and Cora to make a notable mark in life.

Arthur became professor of English at University of Illinois.

Earl was minister in the Methodist church for years.

Lucille married Frank Warren, a missionary to Japan, who later became president of Whitworth College in Spokane, Washington.

Ruth married Lawrence Arksey and served many years as missionary in Mozambique, Africa. In later years they pastored growing churches in Washington.

Fern was professor of music at several colleges in a long teaching career.

Helen was a concert pianist. She married Solon Cronic a business man in Colorado.

Glenna was a defense worker in WWII. and married a farmer, Winton Connor.

Opal married the hired hand, Wilbur Rayner, and raised a fine family on a farm.

The youngest boy, Ted, married a lovely lady, Artha Murray, and took over the homestead farm after Grandfather died. Their four children were raised in the big house that was built years earlier. The house burned down following World War II.

<u>Mildred</u> Lived her life from the very beginning in the Cherokee Strip. She started out teaching a one room school. She married the farm lad who promised to take her away from it all.

Mildred is typical of the vast number of women who were faithful to God and to their families through three of the greatest Social and economic crisis of the twentieth century. It is Mildred's story that prompted this book.

Follow the Daughter of the Cherokee Strip through the great depression, the dust bowl days, and World War II.

Daughter Of The Cherokee Strip

James Secord, the pioneer to the Cherokee Strip was nearly forty years old when he married Cora Belle Surface. She was a lady of twenty three summers at the time.

Their first child. Arthur was born in Dec 1891 The second child, Mildred, was born March 1893. The two children with the parents made the run into the Cherokee Strip in September of 1893. It is Mildred's powerful life story that is central to this book.

This part of her story is taken from her own memoirs:

There were very few trees on the property. My first memory was going with my brother, Arthur, to pick up buffalo chips that the family used for heating and cooking. If the chips were dry they made a quick hot fire.

Coldwater creek ran by on the East Side of the homestead where the horses and cows could drink. It did not flow all year around. Father Secord dug a well but the water turned out so bitter that even the livestock did not like it. Water for drinking and cooking had to be hauled from a neighbor's well where the water was good.

Many of the settlers built houses called soddies. They were cut out of the Prairies sod in sections and piled one on another until the walls were over six ft high. Long poles from trees were laid across the top for rafters. There were not many trees on the prairies. They were not very large and poles from them were not straight.. The rafters were covered with sods like shingles. The Soddy was warm in winter and cool in summer, but they did not last long.

Father had some savings from his school teaching. He bought lumber at Pond Creek, which was a day's drive by team and wagon. He would load the wagon and buy needed groceries. He would spend the night there and drive home the next day. I got so excited when father came home from town with the load of things from the big city so far away.

He built a clapboard house with 12 inch boards running vertically and then batting the cracks with a piece of lath. They found some flat rocks in bluffs above a creek bed for foundation stone. The house was a two room structure with a shingled roof. As the family increased another two rooms were added and all the interior was plastered.

The prairie sod was matted from the old buffalo grass. It was a tough job to break up the prairie to plant crops. A special Steel Plow with vertical as well as horizontal blades helped to turn the stubborn sod.

It was pulled by a team with the driver walking behind holding the handles. This was slow work. A man with a team worked hard all day to do one acre.

The Virgin soil had to be broken up with harrows and

leveled for planting. When it rained a lot the soil became real muddy. When the dry weather came the soil was real hard. The first few years were quite dry and the crop was small.

Father planted Kaffir Corn. We ground up the white Kaffir corn and made mush for cereal. Then we learned we could pop it like popcorn on top of the stove. We had a couple of milk cows and three horses. The cows provided milk and cream, butter and cheese for the family.

As more land was plowed, the settlers discovered that wheat did well in that climate. Wheat could be planted in the fall which provided winter pasture for the livestock. Then it became the cash crop in the summer with a ready market for it. At first the wheat was cut with a scythe and bundled by hand. Then when dry it was threshed out by hand.

When more land was put to wheat, a header machine would cut the wheat into a large wagon called a header barge. Then it was carried to a central place and piled in a large stack. After it was dry a large threshing machine could be hired to thresh the grain and stack the straw. This procedure made it possible for the farmers to raise thousands of bushels of wheat and brought better times.. The prairie country became known as the nations bread basket.

Father and mother worked very hard. They were very devout in their faith. Every morning and night father would gather his family together and read from the Bible and pray for each one of us and thank God for his many blessings.

Two years after the run I remember traveling with my parents back to Topeka Kansas in our covered wagon. Baby Earl had joined our family that year. We were going to visit mother's father, Noah Surface. It was a 250 mile journey of ten days. I was bored with so much travel and it was raining. I discovered as I lay under the canvas canopy that when I put my finger up to the canvas the water would come through. It was fun until I got wet.

Arthur was a year and half older. We played a lot together but he liked to tease so much. I tried to tell my mother on him but she had a baby to care for. I learned that I was no longer the baby of the family and must act like a big girl.

It was a new experience for us to have a grandpa. My mothers father was of Pennsylvania German extraction. He married Sarah Catherine Ridenour in Eaton, Ohio in 1867. Cora Belle, their oldest child was born a year later. Noah Surface fought in the union army. The government gave veterans an opportunity to homestead in Kansas.

In 1869 he loaded his household goods and family on a flatboat and floated down the Ohio River to St. Louis. At that point he bought a team of oxen and a covered wagon and headed west to Topeka. He found a homestead thirty miles south of Topeka at Lyndon. The soil was rich but the land was rocky. By making fences out of the rocks in the field he was able to make a suitable farm with lots of fruit trees.

In Kansas three more children were born, Ida May, John, and Clarence. After Clarence was born, Sarah came down with Consumption (TB). Noah heard that Florida climate would be better for his sick wife. He took his family to Key West, Florida. He lost her anyway and buried her in Florida.

We know very little of this mystery lady in the family tree. The only picture that we have of her at nineteen years of age shows that Cora Belle looks like her.

Cora Belle was nearly thirteen at the time. Upon her came the full household responsibilities for her father and three younger siblings. Noah took his motherless brood back to Kansas. Two years later he married a lady with four children of her own. The melded family of eight worked out quite well.

Noah Surface was a lay preacher. He helped establish several churches in that area. He wanted his daughter, Cora Belle, to have an education. He sent her to Neosho Rapids to an academy. A Bachelor teacher at the academy was James Monroe Secord. She was twenty three and he was Forty. Just right! They married.

Now five years later they went back home with three children in a covered wagon. It was the only visit they ever made to Cora Belle's father who was only six years older than her husband.

While in Kansas my parents were real busy canning and drying apples and peaches to take back to Oklahoma. The trip home was uneventful but tiring. They had been gone over a month. Father's sister, Lenora, lived south of their homestead and a brother, George Secord lived a mile northeast. This provided some care over the property while we were gone.

Father loved trees. His homestead had very few. Right from the start he began to plant fruit and walnut trees. He planted grapes, apples, peaches, and apricots which took a few years to start producing.   The native fruit was wild sand plums, which made terrific jellies. We found some along the creek east of us.

Twenty-five miles south in the sandy soil nearer the Cimarron River the farmers wanted to clear the Jack Oak trees to plant watermelons. Those who cleared the land could have lots of free firewood. He went with his wagon and horse team a days journey. He spent the night in the wagon, loaded it up the next day with poles, and came home the third day. These poles then were sawed up by a hand held cross-cut saw into stove wood lengths. This solved the problem of heat after the buffalo chips were gone.

The first autumn that this was done, father brought home several bushels of black walnuts that were still in the green husk. He piled them on the sunny side of the house to dry out. We had a dog named Ned. Ned found that the green walnut husks were heating up because they were still green. The pile of warm nuts made a nice warm bed at night.

One night Ned was barking and making a lot of fuss. Father got up, put his clothes on and took a lantern out to see what was the matter with Ned. He found that Ned had killed a rattlesnake that had tried to share the warm bed of nuts. Father congratulated Ned for his bravery and went back to bed. The next morning Ned was dead from a Rattlesnake bite.

There were lots of rattlesnakes on the homestead in the early days. Out on the grassland prairie dogs had built their dens under the turf. They had underground burrows that connected one hole to the other. At any time of the day you could see a Prairie dog standing guard on his dirt mound that he had dug from his den. When danger approached the sentinel would yap and thump a warning. All the colony would disappear into their under ground tunnels.

Horses sometime running across the prairie would step into a hole and break a leg that rendered him helpless. Rattlesnakes and owls seemed to be in cahoots with the prairie dogs. This gave place for rattlesnakes to hide out as well as the owls. I don't know what the prairie dog got in return, but they seemed to be friends.

One of the settlers learned the hard way about the rattlesnakes in a prairie dog den. The settlers hated the snakes and tried to exterminate them. This particular settler stepped on the tail of a rattlesnake as it slithered into a den. The wily snake wriggled around in a tunnel to a hole behind the man and came up on his blind side and bit his leg. Some of those snakes were pretty long. With no doctors near, many died from the bites.

The Star School House

A schoolhouse was built out of sod just across the pasture from us. It was in the same section but on the far side so that the school was a mile from our house. It was called the Star school. Five years later, by the time I started to school my father helped built a frame schoolhouse. It had one large room to accommodate all eight grades with one teacher.

Arthur was older so I had some one to lean on at first. Then as we grew to be the bigger kids in school, we would improvise the games that we played at recess. We used the old soddy for a fort and fought many battles. This was more fun as you got bigger. In nice weather girls would bring rag dolls and other things for a playhouse in the old soddy. The boys often times delighted in tearing down our play house so that this did not last too long.

We played games like "Ante Over", "Blind Man's Bluff", or "Steal Sticks". If anyone could afford a ball or make a ball out of town string we would play baseball or a game called "One old Cat". That game was played with three or more children. The one who owned the ball got to pitch. He threw it to the batter who, if he hit it, had to run to a certain base and back before the pitcher could pick up the ball and throw it back to the catcher. If the batter made it back in time, he could bat until he made an out. Then the pitcher would bat and the catcher pitch. This game was better if many played because it was easier to get the batter out and nearly everyone got a turn at the bat.

When they built the school there were some shingles left over. We played "Swat" with them. Each player got a shingle to defend himself, but also to sneak behind another and swat his behind before he could protect that area with his shingle.

We invented a game called 'Shimy". We drew a large square in the yard with a stick. Each of the four corners had a person to defend his corner with a stick. A person who was IT would hit a tin can with a stick into a corner. If the defender allowed the can to stop in his corner then he had to be IT. The one hitting the can was the conqueror of that corner. It was a rough game.

We had no regular playground equipment. We made up games and rules and had lots of fun anyway. It was obviously more fun for the older ones than for the younger children.

After the frame building was built at Star school, my parents started a Sunday school there. Over in the next School district called Canyon Ridge, there was also a church started. A family of Enterlines lived there and one of them was a preacher who held meetings at the schoolhouse. Many times father and mother would drive over there to help with revival meetings.. These meetings were well attended by all the people.

One night our parents took Arthur, baby Earl, and me to the revival. It was dark and so far away that we children fell asleep. The folks hitched the horses to a post and left us in the wagon sound asleep. When the service ended they could not find the horses and wagon Some boys evidently pulled a prank and loosened the reins during the service. There was great excitement generated about what had happened.

The folks caught a ride home with another family. When they turned in to their own place; there were the horses still hitched to the wagon with their heads in the top door of the barn. The children were all still asleep on the floor..

Once a revival was held at the Star school and many people were converted. One of them was my neighbor girl, Thanie Skaggs. She was very concerned about her classmates at the Star school. She would hold services at recess and all the children would play *Church*. Thanie was the preacher and tried to get the children *"Saved."* Since this produced better behavior among the children, no one thought of objecting about playing revival at school.

Thanie developed a goiter while still a young girl and died. Several in her family also died with the same problem. They did not know what caused it like we do now.

The one advantage I had was that father loved music. A Free Methodist church was organized and a building built on a road a mile from the house. Father and mother both could sing well and read notes. Father started a singing school at the church. He had a tuning fork and got the right pitch from it and then led the singing by note.. Arthur, Earl, and I all learned to sing at this school before we had any accompaniment. Father always yearned to play a piano but never had an opportunity to learn.

When I was ten years old, I came home from school one day to find that my father had bought a piano. He brought it out from Pond Creek in a lumber wagon. It was so beautiful and I got first chance to learn to play. Father sat down with me every day and helped me. As soon as I learned to play a little, he would come in from the field and listen to me play. My younger sisters were all envious of me, especially when I got to play while they did the dishes after supper. Several of my younger sisters became very proficient pianists, especially Helen and Fern.

When I finished the eighth grade there was no high school yet in the community. I was sent to Tonkawa fifty miles away from home where there was a preparatory school. Father found a family in Tonkawa where I was able to work for my board and room. I was able to attend four winters there and got a diploma which was much more than most of my girl friends my age. My brothers, Arthur and Earl, went away to high school and college at Greenville, Illinois.

I was needed at home so that my education was somewhat sporadic. I was nineteen when I graduated from prep school. With Arthur and Earl gone to college I stayed home a year to help with the farm. Lucille and Ruth were several years younger but we were all involved with the outdoor work that year. We helped plow fields, harrowed, and planted the fall wheat. We three girls topped the Kaffir corn that year. We hitched a team to a wagon and we would start the team down a row, while we topped the kaffir corn with 12-inch corn knives. We each cut a row and threw the heads in the wagon while the horses walked slowly up the row.

The only opening for unmarried ladies of my age was to find a one-room school. I needed a teachers certificate to teach. There was a teachers college at Alva. In March, father drove me to Carrier where I rode a train for the first time. It took me to Avard. Another train took me to Alva arriving about four in the afternoon.

I knew no one and felt awfully alone. A friend had given me the name of a lawyer in town. I found his office in the small town and he was very kind to me. He knew a lady who kept boarders. He drove me to the depot in his wagon to get my trunk, and then took me to the boarding house. I stayed there and attended college until the end of May.

I went home for harvest. I helped cook for harvest hands until summer school started in July. While I was home the three of us older sisters decided to go to Hillsdale congregational church for a Sunday night service. There were no boys our age in the church our folks attended. We heard that there was a good group of young people at the Hillsdale church.

That was the first time I ever saw a young bachelor farm boy, Jesse Wayman. Jesse Wayman apparently only came to the service to survey the girl crop in that place. He had his hopes on one of the young ladies who was already spoken for. She did not give him the time of day nor did he to us. We all went away disappointed.

Before I went back to the summer school in Alva, father heard about the Fairview School needing a teacher. He took me over to see the school board chairman. Sam Wayman was in the field binding wheat with his son, Jesse. Whether Jesse had any influence with the hiring process I don't know. I was hired at Thirty Dollars a month to start in October.

Fairview school was built in 1898. It was located on a corner of a farm four miles east and three miles north of Goltry, Oklahoma in Garfield County. I went to Alva College for the summer session. I got a teachers permit in September. I came home to take up the awesome responsibilities as the new school 'marm' (as she was called) at Fairview School. I was twenty years old. I was naively eager to take this challenge. I had taken care of nine siblings at home

24

as the oldest girl and I had undergone a highly disciplined lifestyle in rugged circumstances.

The first day I put on my best smile and best dress and went early to be ready. I rang the bell and twenty-eight children mobbed me from every direction. Some walked a mile and a half, some came by horseback, or in a horse drawn buggy. There were older boys bigger than I who still had not finished requirements of the eighth grade.

Five children of regular intervals in ages were Sam Wayman's children, and another Wayman family or two I couldn't tell for sure. There was no phone, no janitor, no man to call on, no nurse, no play ground supervisor, no substitute, no Principal to call on. There were two Outhouses and a horse barn to maintain. The paltry salary had no thought in my mind that day, as a million dollars would not help to allay the insecure apprehension of the moment. I bluffed like I was in charge.

Parents on the prairies expected a lot from the teacher, but they always backed the discipline that was needed. I was glad when the first day was over. I found a place to board and room with a farm family a quarter mile walk north of the school. The school had a piano, I did what my parents did I played a hymn every morning and read a scripture. The farmers thought that was a bonus to have a teacher who could play hymns and lead singing.

The rest of my story took so many directions that I need others to assess it that are the products of my life work. I never thought of myself as accomplishing much. I did the best I knew how and trusted God to do the rest. I know many children touched my life, the Secord family, the Wayman family, school children, church children, neighbors with lots of children, then twelve children of my own and many grandchildren. I can't think of a one of them that I would have wanted to live without.

The Country School House

Fairview school house located in the Cherokee Strip was built in 1898. It was on a one-acre corner of land four miles east and three miles north of Goltry, Oklahoma. This is the school Mildred Secord taught in the school year 1913-14. Also where Mildred's children attended. Vacated in 1936, it was still standing fifty years later.

Lonely she stands beside the road.
I remembered as I passed through.
I stopped to walk down memory lane
from a school boys point of view.
Within its darkened halls I peered
Among the teaching props:
I saw oak desks where pioneer sons
Carved their initials upon the tops.

Sunbeams streamed through broken panes
showed on well worn floor.
It revealed a piano of ancient vintage.
Beside the platform door.

I envisioned a pioneer school marm
With quiet and noble mien
Controlling well with rod and rule,
An orderly learning scene.

There's the timid first grade class.
Reciting the ABC's
Mingled with the eighth grade class
Engaged in spelling bees.
Six more grades in between
To correct and instruct all day,
To meet the expectations of the state
For thirty dollars of monthly pay.

No plumbing, no janitor, no telephone,
No man on whom to call,
Except for a proposal from a farmers son
To take her away from it all.

Like a symbol she stands beside the road
even though the children have grown.
She crumbles away in loneliness now
When many students she had known.
A long time ago the last class closed,
Her purpose of being is gone.
But the principles the school marm taught
Helped make a nation strong.

Phil Wayman   1st grade Class 1928-29

Head Of The Tribe Of Jesse

The nation's breadbasket procured in the Louisiana Purchase was largely passed over by the early settlers who crossed the vast prairies en route to the west coast. In all fairness, the land wasn't empty. Indian tribes lived off the land as nature provided without a fence or a field of grain.

Earth was Mother, and to plow a field was like mutilating your mother as the Indian tribes were driven out and placed on reservations, the farmers took over.

It is not intended to debate the ethics of either side. No matter what one may decide for himself, it will be contested by another.

(Jesse & Mildred wedding picture)

Our purpose is to share how it was and not to just fantasize of what might have been. Emigrants came to pursue the great American dream of freedom to own and enjoy the fruits of labor as God may allow.

29

Sam Wayman was a son and son in law of emigrants from England. His parents, Joseph and Elizabeth came from Cambridgeshire, England to New Orleans in 1845. They were newlyweds wanting to start their lives together in America. Elizabeth's older brother, John Carter, was also on the same ship. He was a widower with four children who accompanied him on the voyage.

Joseph Wayman and John Carter were compatible in-laws who stayed together. They moved upriver and settled in Clay County, Illinois. With his first family grown, John Carter married Sarah Pointer, a much younger lady. Sarah Pointer Carter mothered nine children.

Joseph and Elizabeth Wayman had eight children. Following the civil war, Elizabeth died leaving her young children motherless. Like so many pioneer women she lies in an unmarked grave somewhere in Clay County, Illinois. Joseph found a widow lady, Nancy Brown, as his second wife and mother for his large family.

In the early seventies the Cheyenne Indian tribe was forced on reservation that freed large sections of southern Nebraska for homesteading. Joseph & Nancy took their eight children and John & Sarah Carter took their nine children and headed west to take a patent on land. The two families lived on adjacent homesteads north of Holbrook in Gosper County.

Joseph was an itinerant Methodist preacher who held services in school houses or churches while he made his living farming. Since the land was new, the divine services were held in schools or any place a group could be gathered. The visiting minister often became the judge and arbiter of disputes in the communities. Homespun wisdom emanated from the preaching points.

One story that comes down to us is worthy of passing on. When the Itinerant preacher came to one of his preaching points one Sunday, he met a farmer who was quite upset. Someone had stolen his steel plow that was used to break up the prairies. The preacher consoled him that he would find out who did this.

On preaching Sunday, everyone whether saint or sinner was expected to attend. In the course of the service the preacher made the announcement:

"Mr. Brown says someone stole his plow. I'm sure God knows who did it."

"Now I'm going to pray and ask God to show me who did it."

"When He tells me who did, I'll throw the song book at him."

"Let's everybody bow your heads; close your eyes while I pray."

The preacher started to pray, he opened his eyes and looked. A fellow on the back seat had his eyes open. He picked up the song book to throw at him. The fellow ducked. The preacher pointed at him and shouted:

"You're the one who did it. Now come and repent and give farmer Brown back his plow. God will forgive you and so will we."

The pioneer Wayman and Carter families were very close both by location of their homesteads and also socially. Two of the Carter girls married Wayman boys. They were first cousins. John Carter was much older than Joseph Wayman but they died nearly the same time. Both are in well-marked graves in Miller cemetery a few miles north of Holbrook, Nebraska. John Carter's wife, Sarah, lived many years with a daughter Mary Carter Brobst in Goltry, Oklahoma. Sarah died during World War I (WWI) and is buried at Karoma Cemetery.

Samuel Wayman was the eighth child of Joseph and Elizabeth Wayman. He married cousin Amanda Carter in 1881. Samuel was nineteen and Amanda was only fifteen. They farmed for many years in Nebraska in Muddy Precinct. Seven girls and four boys were born in Nebraska.

Samuel was a restless man and wanted to move to better climate. He heard about Oklahoma land in the Cherokee Strip that could be bought for very little.

He had very little. He and his older brother John who also married a cousin Martha Susan Carter decided in 1905 to scout out the Cherokee Strip country. They found farms near the Fairview School that were for sale cheap. They returned to Nebraska, loaded up their large families and started out for Oklahoma.

Samuel and Amanda brought along their eight underage children along with two married children and spouses. John Wayman and Martha had four children. It looked like a whole tribe as they moved along the dirt roads 350 miles through Kansas in four covered wagons loaded with household furnishings, children and foodstuff for a twenty-day journey. There was not enough room for the older boys to ride. Sam's fifth child, Jesse, was fourteen at the time. He walked all the way.

Sam's younger children got to go to Fairview School, which was three-fourth of a mile walk from the house. Sam took advantage of the fact that his corn field lay toward the school house. In the spring the children would hoe a row of corn on the way to school and then hoe a row back at night. In the fall as the school started again, the children helped shuck the corn the same way. This way the farm work was done mostly by hand.

Sam and Amanda had to work from early childhood. They never had time or inclination to pamper children. When the country school amalgamated with the town schools, it became necessary to have a bus to take the children so far. Grandpa opposed it vigorously. "By Dad" (as close to swearing as he ever got) "they want money to buy a bus fer them kids to ride to school, then they tax us again to build a gym so they can get exercise."

By the fall of 1913 Sam Wayman was chairman of the country school board. The school board job was usually anyone who would take it. Sam and Amanda added another daughter and a son to their family after coming to Oklahoma. He had more children at Fairview than any other family.

It was a problem to find a school marm who could teach and harder still to keep her there. Some bachelor farm boy found the teacher a good choice for a wife. After one year at the school with such a large group of various ages, she was usually willing.

Oklahoma became a state in 1906. The requirements for schooling were increased to the eighth grade or eighteen years old, whichever occurred first. So many of the big boys did not care to work on the farms anyway so there was no incentive to pass the grade. It was easier to hassle the teacher who usually was barely out of high school.

Sam Wayman had little time to begin the search for a teacher in summer 1913. The wheat was coming on and he needed to get into the fields and harvest. He had managed to obtain one of those new binders that would cut and bundle the stalks into sheaves. Another person with twine had to bind the bundle and place in shocks to dry. Later models of the Binder had an automatic knotter that tied the twine right on the sheaf before dropping it on the field.

The older Wayman children were married and Jesse was now twenty-one. Jesse was his main help in harvest. His three younger brothers were still too young to be much help. Jesse had worked with his father closely since coming to the Cherokee Strip. His education stopped when he left Nebraska. He worked full time with the farm through seven years of hard work and toil. He had a strong body and a willing spirit. Since Jesse was now twenty-one he was ready to find a wife and farm his own land.

The Hofsommers were a pioneer family living a few miles east of the Wayman farm. This family had a eligible daughter who Jesse liked a whole lot. He could not get adequate opportunity to pursue his desire. He discovered however that the Hofsommer family was faithful attendees at the Hillsdale Congregational church. He hitched the best horse to the buggy one Sunday Night in June to attend the Evening service at the Hillsdale church. The favorite method of courting was to see the lady safely home after dark.

Mildred Secord and her two younger sisters also hitched their best horse to the family carriage to attend the Hillsdale Congregational church. They thought perhaps that eligible young men might be there. The boys were scarce at their own church.

Jesse and Mildred exchanged only glances as Jesse had tunnel vision for the girl he came to see. To his dismay he saw a ring on her finger and a young man escort at her side. The rest of the evening was ruined for him. He went home deeply disappointed. Mildred Secord went home disappointed also.

James Secord heard about a teaching opportunity at Fairview school. He took Mildred in the buggy and drove seven miles to the area. By inquiry he found out that the chairman of the school was Sam Wayman. He found Sam Wayman's farm located on coldwater creek. The gentleman was out in the field binding wheat. His son, Jesse was shocking the bundles.

James and Mildred drove out to the field. Sam Wayman stopped his binder and came over to talk. James introduced his daughter who would like to teach the school this fall. Jesse stopped shocking the wheat and came over to see what was going on. Mildred recognized him immediately and Jesse acknowledged that they had met.

The time was right, the job was right and the social structure was right. She got the Job. Sam Wayman was pleased to have the vacancy filled so quickly. James Secord was pleased to have solved Mildred's future as a teacher. Mildred was doubly pleased.

She found a school to teach and the added bonus of an eligible young man as son of the school chairman who hired her.

Four of the children at Fairview school that fall were Jesse's siblings. Mildred boarded at a farm house a quarter mile north of the school. As winter came on Jesse found occasion to take the younger children to school on cold mornings and pick them up at night. One day Mildred dropped her glove incidentally as she got close to the school house. Jesse found it and brought it to her. Courting was very proper.

Jesse was going on twenty-two and wanted to get out on his own. He was able to rent a farm in January He had a team of horses and a few head of other livestock but was still living at home. He went to harness a team of horses to do some early work on his farm. One of the horses slipped on the icy ground and fell on him breaking his leg. The doctor came out to set the leg. He used no anesthetic. Four men were required to hold Jesse down while the Doctor put the splintered leg in place.

Mildred found occasion to drop by to offer some sympathetic care which Jesse liked very much. Before he was back on his feet the romance bloomed. When the love bug bites, everybody has to get out of the way because it bites without reason.

Early in March an event occurred that provided the impetus needed to get her away from it all.

Mildred opened each school day by playing a hymn and reading a scripture. No one objected as Bible stories were part of the reading assignments.

This particular day she called up the fifth grade history class while the rest of the school studied assignments. The county superintendent made his annual visit that day and entered without knocking. Mildred was auditing the fifth grade history lesson. She did not see him take an empty seat in the rear.

Midway through the lesson she noticed this gentleman in her room. She was too shy and embarrassed to talk to him. One of the students asked a question. "What was the Alamo?" Mildred could not remember but was afraid to say she did not know with this strange man present.. She guessed; "it was a battle of the Spanish Armada." As she finished her class she noted the man had gone. She found a note on the desk. "Better bone up on your history," signed by the county superintendent of public schools.

She interpreted this to mean that she would not be hired again. The school was out in two weeks. She rushed into marriage. Jesse and Mildred took the train to Enid on the 20th of March and were married by the Justice of the Peace. This was a keen disappointment to Mildred's parents who would have frowned on any marriage outside of the church.

As I assess the situation and knowing what a brilliant woman mother was, I doubt that Fairview school would consider the blunder a cause for letting her go. Most of those people didn't know history of any kind. If I didn't know about the Alamo, I would think her answer was a pretty good guess.

Jesse Wayman inherited a penchant for hard work. He had no tolerance for dishonest gain or laziness. All his life he was involved with sheer survival, and the only solution was hard work. In Nebraska there was a Muddy Creek and they lived in the Muddy Township. To get up early was a "muddy start". Jesse got a muddy start every day. It was an insult to him if a neighbor got into the field before he did or stayed later at night. His ego was high. His ambition was to acquire many farms and get out of the extreme circumstances that he was reared in.

Most of the early farmers calculated a large family an asset like cattle or land. At the close of the first year of marriage a baby girl was born. Almost a year later a boy joined the family. A war broke out in Europe and many relatives had to go away to war. America was kind to the farmers in that food was a strong weapon. Jesse needed his own farm.

During World War I, he bought in his name a cheap farm that others had tried to make a go on. It had four canyons in a 160 Acres of rolling land tucked away a mile on red clay dirt trails. It was unfit for any movable object but cattle.

Jesse bought cows and raised cowboys. Seven children in a row were boys. Jesse also liked hogs. They multiply; and mature faster than cattle. In thirteen years he had lots of hogs, many cattle, A flock of sheep, several horses, chickens, and turkeys and a houseful of seven boys and a girl. Beside his 160 Acres, He rented a hundred acre wheat field from Mr. Constant who was his neighbor on the south.

The year 1927 brought big changes. The dream of empire was stifled by poor production on the poor farm land he owned. He went in debt and bought the 160 Acres adjacent to his farm across the county line to the west. It had a bigger house and bigger barn and better farmland.

That August number nine of the periodic stork visits changed life forever. It was a Girl. Oldest sister, Ruthalie was elated. She had been keenly disappointed in the last few boy types because she hoped for some help in defense of sisterhood. "Sissy" is another story for later in the book.

Early in 1928 with the new farm in wheat, the price was good. The **"roaring twenties"** saw industrial prosperity. The stock market was high. Calvin Coolidge, **"silent Cal"**, was closing a second term as president. Herbert Hoover took over the helm of the Republican Party with unprecedented optimism. **"Two cars in every garage; A chicken in every pot."**

Jesse Wayman believed this, but his experiences with cars made him cautious about the "two cars" part. If he was going to increase farmland, one of the cars should be a tractor. Bankers loaned money for farms and machinery at high interest rates. It was heady business. Jesse reached out and bought on credit a big Case tractor and a huge harvester-thresher and a plow.

The unmuffled roar of the tractor and its huge size intimidated Jesse. He was a horseman. He was raised with horses and handled all kinds and loved the quietness of their conduct in the field. He never enjoyed loud unpredictable vehicles that did not respond to "Whoa". It was here that having a son in the family right away paid off. Dean was a lad of twelve but very mechanically inclined.. Jesse spent a few hours teaching Dean how to operate the tractor. Obviously it was the other way around as Jesse never did learn to run the tractor.

The first harvest with the tractor and combine expanded to include custom cutting of wheat for neighbors. A neighbor manned the combine and Dean drove the tractor. Jesse's effort to haul away the grain with horse and wagon was insufficient to handle the speed of threshing with a combine. He had to hire a truck to haul the grain.

Jesse went back to his row cropping with the horses. This seemed like a good idea. He had other boys that must be kept busy so the farm was both horse powered and mechanical. His optimism paid off for one year. Jesse paid the required payment on his land and machinery after harvest and bought more. **Hoover won the election!**

Model "T" without a Top

My father lived at the transition of two ways of life. He was the fifth child of a large family. His parents had moved from western Nebraska down into the newly opened Cherokee strip at the beginning of the century, Father was a lad of 14 at the time. He walked all the way.

His education stopped at that point as he was considered a full time worker on the homestead..

The method of travel was horseback or the four wheeled buggy pulled by one horse. Father was good with horses and always had several teams to work with. The horse & buggy was the conveyance of courtship of the Fairview Country School teacher. It was the family carriage through the birth of the first two children.

In 1913 Henry Ford put the Model T on the assembly line and made it financially competitive with a horse and buggy. Father wanted one of those. By 1917 the world war brought a measure of prosperity to farmers. Father bought a farm located on a dirt trail. He also that year bought a second hand **1913 Model T.**

He was so proud to drive into the yard with his first car. The top was down because it was summer time. He had mama open the corral gate and the barn door while he carefully parked his **Model T** inside for the night.

The next morning he needed to back the car out so the barn could be used for the horses and cattle. He had learned how to crank it and drive it forward but his limited skills did not include backing the vehicle. After several attempts at the right procedure, he got the car to back up. He was so nervous looking over his shoulder to see where he was going that he could not remember how to stop it.

He hollered "WHOA! WHOA!" He pulled back on the steering wheel. The **Model T** chugged across the corral and backed into a tree at the far end of the corral. The wood staves for the canvas Top that protruded out behind were all broken by the impact.

From that time the family grew from two to three, four, five, and six, all riding in a **Model T without a top**. The only advantage of the horseless carriage was that you could get there quicker. With prairie winds and rain and snow or hot sun we were more disheveled upon arrival.

In February of 1924 with prospect of a seventh child and a good crop, father resolved to buy a new **Model T with a top** on it. New cars were shipped by train in those days in large crates that required assembly at the local garage.

It was a grand day for the six stair-steps of children, when papa came driving down the dirt road in a shiny black and good smelling **Model T with a top** on it. It had side curtains with isinglass windows to look out of. We hardly dared to touch it. Father had built a new garage just the right size to avoid his previous mistake. He carefully parked his car and closed the door for the night.

The next day was snowy and slick afoot, unfit for travel on dirt roads. After chores and breakfast, the desire to show off his new car clouded his judgment. His brother, Richard, lived on the next farm to the east. Now you could travel by horseback less than a mile across the field. The dirt road was three times farther.

Father thought up some excuse for the trip. He took his two oldest sons to savor the experience of a new car. The dirt trail led up through the pasture and then turned onto a road where there was a deep canyon. The previous Model T had a problem of negotiating the steep inclines. Sometimes he would have to back up and get up more speed to climb out on the other side.

Father was in a bind. He needed to descend the canyon with enough speed to make it up the other side first try. The red clay dirt was slick. Somehow he got the front wheel in a different rut than the back ones. He pulled back on the steering wheel. "Whoa up a Little."

Whoever had mounted the steering wheel the day before had forgotten to put the nut on that keeps it in place. When father pulled back on the wheel to "Whoa up a little."The steering wheel came off in his hands. His car left the road and climbed up the bank at the side of the road. It toppled over on its top in the roadway. All the wooden staves that frames the top were broken. By the time father went back down to get his horses to right his car, the battery acid had dripped onto the canvas curtains and eaten away the fabric.

Many more years through wind, rain, snow, cold or heat Jesse Wayman's large family travelled in a **Model T without a top.**

A Mighty Woman Was Mother

The daughter of the Cherokee Strip was seasoned in making do with what was available. She was educated as much as possible for her time and place. She had already endured enough difficult circumstances to develop a patient disposition. She was far ahead in that quality.

Shortly after marriage she experienced a very profound life changing experience with God. She became a very devout lady. On this score she was ahead of her husband also. She never raised her voice in anger but ruled the home in a loving caring manner. She taught Sunday School class at the country church. and attended all the services. Mother taught us to Pray by her own example. She led the family in morning prayers and committed each of us to God who never slumbers or sleeps.

Father did not like to go to church. Father showed us how to work because that's all he knew how to do. He knew certain scriptures. The one about "*if the Ox is in the ditch on the Sabbath, pull it out*" and "*He that does not work, neither let him eat.*" On Sunday morning after chores and breakfast, he would hitch up his team of horses to a wagon and go out to see if there were any ox in the ditch. He would manage to get around by noon and after lunch, spend the rest of the day resting on the Sabbath in proper manner.

Mother was not allowed to drive the car, because women do not understand such things. She could harness a horse and drive the buggy anywhere as good as any man. She observed Jesse driving the **model T** and learned the principals of how to crank it and put it in gear and stop etc. It was frustrating to her. When she needed to go to town or to church he was not available or may not have a mind to take her.

One day Mom needed something at Goltry six miles away. Jesse was in the field far away from the house. She went out and cranked the car and backed it out of the garage and drove up through the pasture praying all the way. She got to the town, bought what she needed and drove carefully back home. Father saw her on the return and fretted but he had to allow mom to drive the car after that. She showed that women can do anything as well or better than he could do it.

She never had an accident with the cars like father did. Father never was good at mechanical things, which was evident in the story of the **Model T without a top**.

Mother knew how to can and preserve everything. When butchering time came she could build a fire outdoors with a large black pot and render the fat into lard. She also made lots of home made soap.

One of the family stories that father loved to tell on mom occurred at butchering time. The children were at school so we have to depend on father's version of what happened.

A neighbor, Walt Vogtlander, came over with his gun to help. Walt shot the pig and father rushed in with the knife to bleed it. The shot stunned the animal briefly. It came to and fled the scene. The pig went right through the fence and around the farmyard; The men in pursuit.

Father called to our hound dog to head him off. The dog did not understand "heading off" but he understood "sic em." Instead of in front to head him off. the hound dog nipped at his back end. The frightened pig took off like a rocket around the sheds, barns and garden. With the dog adding incentives to speed at every turn.

The fat pig headed for the house. Mother heard the commotion and came out to see what it was about. The porker came around the house straight at her. She picked up a ball bat that boys had left in the yard and hit the animal between the eyes. The pig was **Out** at home plate!

Father declares that Mom broke the ball bat over the pig's head. Mama said the bat was already broken. I expect that was the truth; because we never had a good bat to play with. We all liked Father's version the best. We coined the phrase: **A Mighty Woman was Mother, she broke the ball bat over the pigs head and killed it.**

We milked a lot of cattle and sold cream for necessities. We had our own butter and cottage cheese and all the milk we needed for the large family. We had one acre of garden that kept us in vegetables and potatoes. Mother always raised lots of chickens. This provided fresh eggs and fried chicken for family use. Each Saturday mother took cases of eggs to sell along with the cream to the produce house in Goltry. This provided for the necessities that must be purchased at the store. The large family never starved or went a day on welfare like many other families did in that time. I think you could say we were not poor, we just didn't have much money.

Saturday was shopping day in the farm towns. The merchants were happy for Saturday. A big event for any of the children that got to go along was an Ice Cream cone. It was a double dip for a nickel.

Saturday afternoon the town merchants had a Drawing. Tickets were given out at the stores for each quarter of purchase. These were placed in a big cage and spun around. Then someone would draw out a ticket. The name on the back, if present, would be awarded a five-dollar bill for the first one, and then three dollar for next, two dollars for third. There were several one-dollar awards. It was surprising how big a crowd a small town could muster at the Drawing. Every one came out on main street when the announcement was made. Mother with her large family and consequent purchases, came home often with one of the awards.

Mother was a powerful woman as a teacher. She taught school and then Sunday School. She was powerful in prayer. She read the Bible and prayed everyday for her family and others. When the WWII broke out, Uncle Sam reached down for the boys from the ranch. As each boy left for war, mother took her well worn Bible and read the 91st Psalm.

He that dwelleth in the Secret Place of the most high shall abide under the shadow of the Almighty. I will say of the Lord, He is my refuge and my fortress. my God, in Thee I trust. Surely he shall deliver thee from the snare of the fowler, and from the noisome pestilence. He shall cover thee with his feathers and under his wings shalt thou trust. His truth shall be thy shield and buckler. Thou shalt not be afraid of the terror by night; nor for the arrow that flieth by day. nor for the pestilence that walketh in darkness; not for the destruction that wasteth at noonday. A thousand shall fall at thy side and ten thousand at thy right hand, but it shall not come nigh thee.

She then prayed fervently for us.

Three boys joined the Navy and two were in the Army. All went to the Pacific theatre. The boys were in places like the Aleutians, Guadalcanal, New Guinea,

51

Admiralty Islands, Hawaii, Australia, South Seas, Luzon, Panay, Negros, Japan and places God only knows where. All Five came home again. Awesome!

The Lilac Bushes Beside the House

Mother was giving of time and strength to help her family. Rarely did my mother lose her temper. She maintained behavior that would be difficult ordinarily. Beside the house on the first farm there was a row of lilac bushes. The shoots grew profusely and if not pruned would take over the yard.

When the childish behavior reached a point that required action; the culprit would be handed a knife with instructions to bring a lilac. This would give adequate time for self appraisal. The mind realized it was deserved and evoke a promise to not do it again. With a big family of boys, the lilacs were visited frequently. The lilacs seemed to enjoy the pruning and blossomed profusely.

Mother was of adequate proportions but her might was not in the force of correction but was in the skill of administration. Her olfactory nerves were tuned to any harmful experimentation that boys might engage in. Father's family had some strong unsavory habits with drinking and tobacco. Father fortunately did not indulge in either of them.

I remember the powerful lesson that was learned when my oldest brother came from town with a plug of tobacco. He had lied to the store keeper about an uncle requesting it. He showed it off to the rest of us who were considered allies. We all sneaked down into the canyon to test our status as men. We each took a big bite. We swallowed the juice that we accumulated with the first chew. In minutes all five of us were laid out on the canyon floor with a woozy sickness that brought an end to that adventure. Mother knew when to not punish. A bunch of boys without appetite for supper, was all the evidence she needed that we were already suffering for our sins.

The code of the times was that property was in the husband's name. Father had his name on everything and when the purebred hog herd was established it was J.E. Wayman and Sons. The farms were in his name without mention of mom. Later in life father had a stroke and had to be confined to a rest home. Mom had to get a transfer of a farm over to her name so she could do business. It was amazing that father with his mind severely affected signed the papers in the presence of an attorney. Then when father died she had to go through probate and pay inheritance tax to take over all the farms. It was cases like this that brought federal action to raise the limits on inheritance tax and enact community property laws.

Mother followed the scriptural mandate to give a tenth to God's work. Her only money access was the egg and cream money she bought necessities with. Father didn't take kindly to this tithing thing. He had a big family to feed. Actually I doubt that the farm made much money. Father was in debt more than the land was worth. For many years any profit was consumed in interest on the debt.

World War II brought changes to the farm and prices of land. After Fathers death, the land escalated sharply in value. Mother wrote into her will a tithe on the increased value of the land. Mother lived seven years yet and at the time of her death the property was worth considerable. It took two more years to close the estate and pay the tithe. Within a month after the tithe was paid out on the estate, something awesome took place. Lets journey back a little in time to tell you about:

The Men With the Long Black Cigars

Way back in the middle of the depression days some men came out to our farm in a big car and long black cigars. They were oil men. The hope of oil was real as oil was found in several places around us. Father dreamed of the day we would have many oil wells.

The farms were leased by oil companies at $1 an acre. It was enough to pay the taxes on the place in those difficult years. Though others seemed to strike it, we just hoped. In early 60's an oil well pumped on the home place for a while but closed down due to poor productivity and low oil prices. The whole idea of oil was looking more like a fluke as years passed.

In the late Seventies, the estate was settled and the tithe paid. Within a month they struck oil on one of the farms. It pumped for five years while the oil prices ; were the highest in history. Along with that the other farms leased for more per acre than was paid for them originally. Coincidence? I don't think so. In the Bible there is a promise about **bringing all the tithes into the storehouse, and God will open the windows of heaven upon you**. * Mother put into practice what she believed and we were the ones who benefited from it. She was a mighty woman of faith.

* Mal 3:10

Shattering Of The Empire Dream

A new sound invaded the prairies. The roar of the four cylinders and loud 'pop' 'pop' of John Deere tractors joined together as farmers tore up more prairie grazing land. Even the more rolling hillsides were plowed under to raise wheat. The nations bread basket was never so full. The means of enlarging the harvest occurred so suddenly that farms sold for high money. Banks would lend at substantial Interest.

Wheat price was good. Along with wheat pasture in winter came increase in dairy cattle with high butterfat content. Farm families milked their own cows and sold rich cream. This along with the egg money from chickens would provide the few grocery items at town stores. A large garden and butchering times provided most of the food for the family. How could you lose?

Jesse was determined to provide a farm for each son and his daughters would marry farmers. He worked long hours without let up. **His thinker-upper ran fast. His getter-doner lagged, so the hurrieder he went the behinder he got**. His family increased faster than his fortune and then other events beyond his imagination came into his life as an unwelcome guest and lodged in his habitation ever after. I bring you eye witness account as a participant in what happened next.

Father had barely gotten his wheat harvested when the stock market crashed in September 1929. His crop was good that year but the price went way low. The cost to produce the crop was a lot more than he could get for it. OVER PRODUCTION? Who ever heard of such a thing? The people who wore the **Square Cap** had predicted for years that someday the ability to produce food would not be able to keep up with the population boom.

Wheat went to .25 a bushel. He could all of a sudden buy the farms around him for a song and sing off key. Tractors and combines sold cheap as farms foreclosed. The only thing that increased was the size of his debt. **Take That!**

The only thing Jesse Wayman had was his reputation and a hope that next year he'd get a bigger crop and a better price. He went to the banker for more credit for another year . This went on for most of his life.

Politics had promised so they get blamed. It was Hoovers fault! They voted him out in 1932 with just one term. The New Deal was the next promise. The fix was to cut down on acreage so that every farmer raised less grain. Hopefully this would cause the price to go up. The farmers were paid so much for every acre they did not raise wheat on. In lieu of wheat he could raise oats or corn. He did and worked harder than ever.

The payment on farm and machinery must go on. Jesse's philosophy seemed to be; **"Try anything that laid eggs or gave milk or produced a crop or meat for the family**." There was no time or money left for play or vacations or time off for anyone. He owed the profits at the bank that must be at least partially paid so he could borrow for next time.

If you raise sorghum grain and Oats, You need something to feed it to. He increased the hog herd. He took a load of weaning pigs down to Enid to the livestock sale one Saturday. The pigs sold for thirty cents a head. To his dismay when it was time to settle up, the sales fee was a minimum of fifty cents a head. **Take that!**

Along with the depressed prices of the early thirties, came another formidable foe, drought! The big tractor had been employed night and day in harvest time. Harvesting the grain in sunlight and plowing under the stubble at night. This maneuver seemed to make a better crop the next year since the stubble had time to rot in the soil by planting time.

Plowing fields early in June and opening prairies only aggravated the summer heat, which led to less rain in summer. Fields became powder dry. Ponds and streams dried up. Grasshoppers that follow droughts came in droves to eat every green thing. **Take that!**

Cattle prices dropped so that there was little demand for the calves. The herds increased. Then there were too many Cattle for the range land as the grass dried up. Nobody wanted your thin stock because there was so little green grass. Nobody wanted fat stock either. Supply of beef was more than demand. vast unemployment put beef out of reach for families in the cities. **Take That!**

Again the New Deal came to help by shooting some of the thin stock and paying the owners a pittance to lessen the herd size. One depression story that should not be lost to time came out of the above situation with shooting the cattle.

A Man from the big city in the east was hired by the government to come out west and take over the task of shooting the poor cattle that were starving. He started his task and shot one after another of thin stock. He encountered a Billy Goat in the cattle pen. The man was unsure about this fierce looking Billy goat, He ran into the office for advice. He shouted "There an ugly critter out there that has long whiskers and mean look in his eye and smells awful, what shall I do with Him.?" The Head man in the office yelled back "Don't Shoot, that's a Farmer".

The winds that make 100+ degree days bearable whipped across the prairies and the land began to blow. The "**Dust Bowl**" days saw huge clouds of dust that clouded the sun. It piled up at East-West fence rows until you could step across the top wire. It threatened to turn the Cherokee Strip into a desert. In late afternoon when the windstorm subsided, the dust was scooped out of the house to make it livable for another day. **Take that!**

All the farmers were affected by the depression, the drought and dust. Jesse's older brother, Essel, was married already when the whole family came from Nebraska. He came with his bride to make their home in the Cherokee strip country. Essel was more conservative than Jesse. He only had two children, one farm, and less machinery. He played it safe. When the depression struck and the drought came he could not pay the interest on his mortgage either. The banks foreclosed on him and took everything he had to clear his debts. Essel was free. Free as a bird to stand in the bread line and seek any job he could get. He had no hope of anything. The rest of his life he begged for a crust of bread.

Many of the neighbors sold out or lost their farms and joined the Grapes of Wrath crowd that John Steinbeck wrote about in his famous novel. Jesse Wayman would have done the same thing but he was in debt too far to sell out. Is there a level below broke? Yes, it's like Jesse Wayman. Nothing you own comes close to satisfying the creditors.

The land was now worth only a fraction of what he had paid. He had lots of everything including kids and no demand for any of it. Land and machinery like his were selling at farm foreclosures everywhere leaving families with nothing.

The Banker had no hope of retrieving the debt. They had to renew the loan year after year in the same hope that Jesse Wayman had. "Next Year we'll get a bigger crop and a better price." Hope is worth more than money. Hope is like a knot in a rope that the hand can grasp and hold on through another year and the next year and another, on and on.

Depression Children

While the Dust ravaged the farm, not all things were gloom. The home was being set up for some thing only God knew about. When Betty Lucille was born in 1927 there were no more periodic visits of the country doctor to the ranch.

The old iron bed that had survived the perpetual occupancy of nine children for sixteen years seemed to now be ready for retirement. Jesse's younger brother and his wife were still in need of such facility. The iron bed with the white paint (probably lead paint) mostly chewed off was given to the brother's wife where it was used for many years more.

Meanwhile back at the ranch five more years went by. WHOOPS! Another beautiful girl was born. We named her Lida Elaine. Depression or not Vernon Samuel was born two years later. Instead of the caboose coming by in 1927 like we thought, the real caboose came in 1936 with the arrival of a jolly little fellow, Roger Jay. Three healthy active fun loving children.   There were many built in baby-sitters, though I don't remember anyone sitting much.

The older children did not need dolls or toy soldiers to play with. We had real live, mischievous little ones that no toy store or Sears catalogue can duplicate. Life was real.

The Doctor who attended was accustomed to going to the ranch regularly and his fee was $30.00 or farm produce. Through snow or rain or dust or heat the country doctor was subject to call any hour of day or night.   The phones had come in and groups of farmers were hooked up to party line.   When the phone rang at night to the operator in town, neighbors would rubber in to see who was calling the doctor in the night.   No birth announcement was needed.   All the neighbors knew about it before the doctor.   Usually one of those neighbor ladies would be called on to come help out for a day.

When Vernon Samuel was born, Lina Unruh was called to assist. At breakfast the next morning father tried to be magnanimous. He told Lina Unruh in the hearing of all the children, "This has been quite a night. The brood sow had nine pigs and one of the milk cows had a heifer calf and I got another boy all in the same night". It is not known for sure whether the value of each was in the order of his pronouncement, but I would not be surprised.

The years of depression dragged on, the drought continued and the harvest was not much. Jesse Wayman went down to the bank to get the loan extended so he could have something to plant another crop with. The forms were standard with only a few lines to list his dependents. he always had to use the back side of the form. Mama had always done that for him, but he was alone that day. Naming his dependents was difficult task enough without having to remember ages. He started out with the oldest at eighteen, which was right. He thought he had planned his family. He listed them at two years apart. By the time he got to Number nine, he was down to two years old and had three left over and didn't know where to put them.

Nobody was going to count the kids because kids did not count for much. Thank God for America! You can't get put in prison for debts nor sell children to slavery any more.

The Threshing Crew

The Prairie farmers were on the front edge of changes in harvest procedures. For two thousand years crops were raised and harvested much like the Bible days. With the industrial revolution came the McCormick binder, then the header; and then the combined harvester thresher. The ability to harvest large amounts a day was brought into reach of anyone who could afford the machinery.

 Along with the advent of binder and header came the threshing machine. Bundles of wheat, oats or barley could be carried by large hay racks to a stationary place. The stuff could be pitched into the big thresher that separated the grain from the straw and blew the straw into a large straw pile.

With the header the crop was carried by large header racks directly to a stationary location and put into stacks. After drying the thresher was brought to the field and placed between two of the stacks. Men with pitchforks heaved the dry stuff into the threshing machine. In both operations a large crew was needed. Farmers would team up and furnish horses, hay racks, and man power. It took the better part of summer getting every farmer's harvest done.

Young men starting out in life could always find work in the harvest fields. Starting in Texas in May he could follow the wheat harvest north through the plains states clear into Canada. It took about five months. It was always hot, because threshing needed hot, dry weather. Days started away before early and ran to half past late at night.

Jesse Wayman worked harvest all his life. He knew the binder, the header and the threshing machine. He did not know tractors and combines. They were too fast, noisy and complicated. When The New Deal paid farmers to cut back on wheat production, they were allowed to raise oats or barley. In the process the binders became the harvesters again of these crops.

Jesse had nine boys and five of them were suitable harvest hands. He had two teams of horses and two aged bundle racks. Father found a big thresher that someone had discarded years earlier and paid a hundred dollars for it. After our wheat was combined in early June and the tractor was free, we started threshing oats etc. for neighbors for miles around.

Father was an efficiency expert. He found work for his own large family and hired people beside to help us. A neighbor boy, Roy White joined our crew with a team and rack. He was an excellent hand and a hard

66

worker. He worked for the crew several years. Emil Buller was a great spike pitcher who worked on the threshing crew a lot.

A way before early in the morning the stair door would open and father would say one word: BOYS! He expected to hear a thud of feet hitting the floor. I never remember sleeping in after the pronouncement at the stairs door, winter or summer. Father would head for the barn and boys should be there immediately if not sooner. There was a lot to do before a wheel turned in the field. Twenty cows were milked, the hogs fed and water provision made for hot days. The horses were brought in and fed ground oats.

After a hearty breakfast, the horses were harnessed, the machines fueled and greased. By the time the sun started to greet the day with a little heat, It was time to load the racks to begin the threshing.

The hired hands showed up at the time we hit the field. The big tractor was belted up to the thresher. The machinery whirred above the roar of the tractor. The team of horses pulled the loaded hayrack up beside the long feeder. The driver of the team and a spike pitcher unloaded into the feeder at a fast rate. As the bundles were conveyed up the feeder chute, whirling knives cut the twine that held the sheaf together. The loosened sheaf was thrust into the throat of the thresher. The spinning cylinder with claws beat the grain off the stalk. The grain would fall down through a sieve where a big fan separated the chaff from the grain. The heavier grain fell into an augur that conveyed it up to the half bushel measure. When a half bushel by standard weight was achieved, the measure would trip and the grain would be conveyed to the waiting wagon or truck.

The owner took it from there to scoop into a granary. He had to work fast enough to return before the next wagon was full. Once the grain was threshed out of the stalks, the straw was shaken backward to a blower that blew it through a big pipe onto a huge straw pile. Repeat that all morning long.

Promptly at noon the crew headed for the farmhouse where the women provided a thanksgiving size meal for a crew of ten beside their own family. There was fried chicken, mashed potatoes and chicken gravy, lettuce by tub full, peas, or beans, or corn on the cob, tomatoes, or anything in season out of the garden, washed down by gallons of iced tea. Dessert was pie or cake. Repeat the procedure day after day for the threshing season of 24 days except Sunday.

We got to sprawl on the floor for rest after dinner for fifteen minutes. "LET'S GO GET IT!" The Boss hollers. We hitch up the. horses who had been watered and fed a gallon of oats during the noon hour. By now the after noon sun bore down with up over 100 degrees heat. The sweat poured off like water slightly cooling the body with the usual afternoon winds.

The big thresher liked it hot. The stuff would go through better with less chance of choking it down. The beards would get down your neck. The dust settles in and covers your face and clothes until you could hardly bear the day. We hoped for a breakdown of machinery that sometime would happen.

We could then rest in the shade of a wagon for a break while Emil Buller would entertain us. He was so good at his story telling that it made a hot day bearable. Emil was always working for somebody because he had seven children to raise. He never complained. He worked hard and made life more enjoyable with his stories and fun things that he would do when he had a chance.

Emil worked at the machine as a spike pitcher a lot because he could lay the bundles in straight and fast. We found out that Emil was afraid of snakes. We boys in the field killed a bull snake and threw it on the load of bundles where Emil would sure see it. Sure enough, when his fork picked up the long snake on a bundle, Emil yelled with fright and jumped off the wagon and started running across the field. He later joined with us in laughing at himself when he discovered it was dead.

Most of the time he worked for a dollar a day in the depression days, but he got two dollars a day on the threshing crew. As pay day approached after twenty four days of threshing, Emil was heard to say. "I don't know what I'm going to do with all my money."

Other humorous events were provided by a suckling colt that followed his mother around the field to bother her for milk whenever she rested.. One of the boys bragged about his new straw hat how cool it was. He laid it aside in the shade and became engrossed in Emil's story. The colt found the hat and chewed it up to get the salt out of the sweat band.

The colt also found the cool Jug in the tool box of a bundle wagon. He discovered he could pull the cork out with his teeth and get a cool drink of water. Once he discovered this trick the colt was a nuisance with all the water jugs. On the last day of threshing season someone grabbed another man's hat and celebrated by throwing it through the threshing machine. I was amazed to see the hat came through onto the straw pile unscathed.

Father always prided himself in honesty. A half bushel measure was full then he would press it down, shake it, and then run it over so that the farmers would for sure get their money's worth. That was why the neighbors wanted us to thresh their grain. The Bible says that's the way God works with us. He gives us a good measure, pressed down, shaken together and running over.

While we were in the middle of the season one year, we had a breakdown that delayed us getting over to the neighbors field the next day as father had promised. He made mother come to the field and drive him over to the neighbor to apologize. Mother did not see the need to go to all that bother when the neighbor was not too trustworthy with his dealings. Father became irritated with her and said, **"But I gave him my word and my word is all I've got."** The preacher says, "that will Preach!"

The first year on the threshing crew, I was 14. That year was a new thing for all of us and the expectations were not too high. After the season ended on Saturday night, Father took us all down to the little town of Goltry to Bogdahn's drug store. He lined us boys up at the counter and bought us each one our own bottle of Coca Cola, worth .05 in that day. That was our pay for 24 days of harvest. The hired help all got $2.00 a day.

In later years father felt more magnanimous. Every day by mid-afternoon someone would journey to town and buy each one an ice cold bottle of soft drink and allowed us to stop to savor it. Father invented the five minute rest break in mid-afternoon. Of course the afternoons were six hours long.

The work continued until dark when we fed the weary horses and did our chores and showed up at supper for another huge meal. Then half past late at night we could take a dip in the stock tank to cool off and fall into bed. It seems like we no more than hit the sack until the stair well door would open and we'd hear, "BOYS!!"

Addenda: Father had a stroke when he was mid seventies in age. Mother put him in a rest home at Pawnee. That same year my wife, Alma, and I took a break from many years pastoring a church to visit the Holy Land and European countries. We returned by the folks place to visit my father in the rest home.

My brother, Clarence who had stayed with the farm took us up to see him. It was near harvest time and though you could not see a wheat field from the rest home, father knew it was harvest time. As soon as father saw Clarence, he started talking about getting the machinery ready, the granaries ready, and get the crop in early lest a hail storm destroy the crop.

Clarence tried to get his attention focused on us by saying, "Papa, this is your son, Phil. He's been on a long trip to Israel and Europe and he is here to see you" Father studied me a little trying to remember if he had a son, Phil.

A glimmer of recognition shone in his eye and a look of disgust came over his face. He said, **Why did you go away so far in harvest time!** The Preacher again says, "That will Preach."

Sissy

The first child of the tribe of Jesse was a girl. She was named Ruthalie but we all called her <u>Sissy</u>. The next seven children in a row were boys. She assumed a caring roll almost immediately. She was really only a year older than brother Dean, but she was ahead of him in wit and wisdom. By the time Ruthalie was ready for school, she was only five going on six in December. The parents decided that the school house, nearly two miles away, was too much for a small child. Mother taught her to read and write and cipher at home.

The following year, little brother Dean, went with her to the Fairview School. She was far ahead of Dean and all the other first graders. There were no second grade students that year so the teacher placed her in the third grade. She was sharp and stayed ahead of her third grade class. She was only eleven years old when she finished the eighth grade. She entered The Goltry High School in the fall of 1926 and graduated as class salutatorian at Fifteen years of age.

For many years she was the only girl while the family increased to a brother and then to two, three, four, five, six, seven. She was called on early to change diapers, wash dishes and clean up mess. She was the baby sitter whatever that means (no time for sitting). She accepted her role as a second mama way before her time.

She was old enough to catch on when there was prospect of a seventh child in the family. She Hoped for a baby sister. It would be nice to have a help in the kitchen with dishes and clean up and sweeping etc. Or just a playmate that played girl stuff. She was so involved with the process that she just knew it would be a girl. One day, father called the country doctor. All the children were taken to the neighbors for the day.

That evening when she came home, father broke the News, "It's a Boy." Ruthalie ran into the bedroom where mother was and threw herself on the bed and cried with disappointment. When she finally looked at mothers face, there was a tear on her cheeks also. She felt ashamed of herself. She looked at the cute little boy and loved him.

She had given up hope for a change when she discovered the box of baby things being prepared. She had no desire to make a fool of herself again. Even God favored boys in the book of Genesis. She empathized with Dinah who was the only girl among the twelve sons of Israel. She stoically accepted the seventh boy.

In 1927 a profound change came in the family with the purchase of more land and mechanization. The same year, mother was taken to the hospital that Doctor Weber opened in his own home in Goltry. The family stayed home that day while Ruthalie took care of us all. She was now twelve years old. Father drove home that night in his **Model T** (without a top) and parked it in the garage and sought out Ruthalie and told her; **You have a baby sister.** Ruthalie let out a whoop and rushed around the yard like a first time father telling everyone and every thing: **I have a baby sister.**

Sissy was a lot of fun to be with. She could think up lots of keen things to do. As a child she was venturous. She had a cousin that lived two miles west on the country road. She took her little brother Dean and started out for her aunt's place. They got over half mile from the house when the folks noticed them gone. A frantic search began around the farm to no avail. Dean with his shorter legs grew tired and sat down in the weeds beside the road and fell asleep. Ruthalie went on alone for awhile but finally decided the distance was too much, so she went home. She was surprised that anyone wondered about them, she knew where she was all the time.

When the second boy, James, was one year old, the three children went down on a cold March day to play around the barn. They made a playhouse in the hog crate and crawled inside to keep warm. The hog crate had lots of straw in it. The straw did not provide much protection from the bitter March wind. Dean decided to go to the house and get matches to set the straw afire to get warm. Baby James was in the back of the crate.

They heaped the straw in the middle. Ruthalie and Dean were both in the front part of the crate. Dean struck the match. This was so exciting. The straw was dry. It caught readily and was out of control immediately. Dean tried to suppress the blaze while Ruthalie ran to the house for help. The screaming baby was trapped in the back of the crate. Mother rushed down and threw water on the fire. By the time they got James out his wet pants had scalded his legs and left permanent scars Sissy got the blame, even though "Dean was the one who lit the fire;" she said.

When Sissy and Dean started to school, she was much sharper and older and was already assuming mothering role in the family. She tried to protect her little brother from the older boys in the country school. One of the big problems in these places was the older boys having fun at the expense of the defenseless younger ones. Dean was one of the smaller ones so he came in for unwanted attention. Ruthalie tried to step in to defend Dean. This delighted the bullies so much that they never ceased the torment. Dean saw that Sissy's defense was inadequate. He saved himself by siding in with the big boys and joined in turning the torment on Ruthalie. This went on until she realized that discretion was better than valor.

The family transportation to the country school was a four-wheeled buggy. It was powered by genuine horsepower. The harnessed horse was placed between the two shafts and the harness secured to the buggy. The driver had two reins in hands. From the seat of the buggy he called "**giddap**" and away we go. The gaits were varied according to the feeling of the animal that pulled it. A long horsewhip applied occasionally could elicit a change in the speed.

This same buggy was the one used in the courting arrangements of Jesse and Mildred. In those days the slower the pace the sweeter was the way home. The four wheeled buggy seated three thin people. A box area behind the seat made as many spaces as needed when packed like sardines in a can.

The four wheeled buggy served the family every day of school at Fairview for eight years. I was only privileged to have this experience in the first grade. By the time I was allowed to join the scholars, there were five of us boys. The older ones got to sit in the seat and drive the horse. The two miles to school was against the north wind.

The prairies offer little comfort from the wind that blows furiously at times. On the prairies there was very little between us and the north pole except a barb wire fence. The smaller boys covered them selves with a lap robe and huddled together in the box behind the seat. This provided some respite on cold mornings.

The old Buggy could be pulled around by putting one person in the shafts and the rest push. The ranch house was on a hill. The hill sloped down to the corral and the barn. Who knows who thought it up, it seemed a keen idea. We could push the buggy up to the top and jump on for the ride down hill. The problem was that someone had to hold the shafts under each arm and steer the buggy downhill. Sissy being the oldest was given the assignment to be the *horse*. It was an exhilarating ride down hill for all but the *horse*. As the buggy went fast and faster the corral gate got closer, the horse jumped out of the shafts and let the buggy crash into the corral gate. The wood shafts broke and the gate was so damaged it never closed easily after that. Father had to cobble together the shafts for use for the school year. He used a piece of wood and baling wire. Father could fix anything if baling wire could do it.

Sissy started Goltry High School at age of eleven. She had to walk a mile across the county line to catch a bus. It had solid rubber tires that provided a jarring ride on bumpy dirt roads. The canvas flaps on the sides rolled up in summer and were rolled down in the winter. It cut the wind but not the cold. There was no heater. In snowy cold morning the bus could not go as well as the horse and buggy. The red clay dirt roads are slick and muddy when wet and rough when frozen. The horse and buggy could go in any weather.

Sissy was so young that she went through some difficult situations trying to be as grown up as the others in her class at school. The first year she went to high school, she had to walk almost a mile through the canyon and up over the hill to catch a school bus. The boys took the buggy and went the other direction to the country school. Sissy must dress warmly in such weather for so long a walk to the bus. Appropriate dress for girls included long handled underwear and cotton stockings. Some of the popular girls in high school wore silk stockings. That's far too cold for our farm girl who had a mile to walk to the bus and four miles further riding an unheated vehicle.

She was so embarrassed with her long underwear in the freshman class. She found a hollow tree down in the canyon on the way to the bus. She would leave house in proper attire. In the canyon out of sight she partially undressed in the cold mornings and stuffed the long handles and the cotton stockings in the hollow tree. Then in the evening, put them on before showing up at the house. Peer pressure is a mindless motivator.

I'm ashamed of this story on Sissy. It seemed like such a good thing at the time. In her struggle to be like the older girls in her class at the town school she had expressed envy for adornments like bracelets or rings. This kind of thing came under the classification of worldly adornment at our house. They were frivolous things that were not to be worn by decent folks. That did not appease the desire for them.

We boys got home from school near Christmas time to discover that father had butchered a fat hog. I don't know who thought this up but it seemed like a keen idea. We got the tail of the butchered animal and fashioned it in a circle like an arm bracelet. We wrapped and wrapped it in all the finest Christmas wrapping we could find until it was a sizable looking present.

We were all on hand as we gave her a gift from all of us. She seemed dubious at first, because we had never given her anything but trouble. As she unwrapped and unwrapped she finally could feel the outline of the circled pigs tail through the layers of paper. "Could it be? Yes it is true, it is a bracelet!" She hurried the unwrapping process almost screaming with delight as she got closer to her trove. The last paper fell away and there was the pig's tail in a circle.

It wasn't the code to cry, but it hurt too much to laugh. Of course we all had a good laugh at her expense, and fun retelling it through the years. Like one of us said, "That was more fun than watching Pa shoot the tax Collector." Shame on us for thinking either of those situations humorous.

Sissy graduated from High school with honor. She was so young, there was no place to go. She had no prospect of college which she would have liked. She spent two more years on the farm where she was sorely needed.

She was in the 4-H Club as most of the rest of us later were. She won a trip to 4-H Club Encampment at Stillwater A-M College one summer. She saw a young man there who had been in her high school years before. His folks had operated a store in Goltry a few years earlier but now lived at Edmond, Oklahoma. They somehow got reacquainted like young folks do. There were letters and then there was announcement of this young man coming to see us on the farm.

It was a day to be long remembered when a gentleman by the name of LeRoy Heffner came to see us. We had a windmill on the farm that served as a great lookout. When you climbed up you could see for miles in the prairie country. We saw this strange car coming up our road a mile away. We were able by word of mouth to make known to all the inhabitants of the ranch that company was coming. Into our yard came this big black expensive Buick car with a prosperous looking driver. The dogs barked, the roosters crowed, and seven boys all went out to meet him when he came. I'm sure no girl ever met her boyfriend with such a cadre of protectors. We all liked him immediately because he seemed to like us.

Ruthalie invited him into the parlor and all boys got chairs and formed a semi-circle around him. Father had an expression for it, "we Paralyzed his face." We had all kinds of things to show him and waited for opportunity to say so. Ruthalie introduced each of us as though we were an important part of this scene. He seemed genuinely interested in the boys. Come to find out, he did not have any brothers in his family and thought it a plus to gain some.

We boys were keenly disappointed when LeRoy asked Ruthalie if she would like to go to town with him. She said , "yes". He didn't offer us to go along. His big car had lots of room, with the whole back seat unoccupied. We were forced into the background with his ploy.

After a few more occasional visits to the farm, we were able to show him all the keen things we had on the ranch. Horses, cattle, hogs, sheep, chickens, turkeys, the old homestead house on the east place, barns and sheds, the canyons, the wheat fields and pasture land, the big tractor and combine and machinery of all kinds. It was like a trip to the zoo.

Instead of coming to help us, he proceeded to marry our choice help and took her away. She left us with a big bunch of boys and two little sisters. All together they could not fill the vast vacuum that was Sissy.

Ruthalie and LeRoy lived in Edmonds a number of years. He worked for the State and Ruthalie fulfilled a dream of college by attending Central Teacher's College in Edmond. Their first child was a **boy** named Jim. Then after three years another **boy**, David, joined the family. Prior to the outbreak of WW II Leroy moved his family to Los Angeles where he worked at Lockheed through the war years and after. Ruthalie was able to finish her education and became a school teacher.

Their move to California was so providential for the Wayman boys who entered the WWII. All of us found a home away from home because we all trained in Southern California. We could visit there on a week end pass. They were a great blessing to us.

The 1927 event of getting a little sister was repeated in 1947. As a second mother to a passel of boys on the ranch and then mother to two boys of her own, she had resigned herself to a life with boys. A late comer was due to arrive. As Ruthalie came out of the effects of the anesthetic she asked the doctor, "What was it?" The doctor said, "You have a fine little **girl**." She grabbed his arm and said; "Oh, Thank You, Doctor, Thank you, Doctor." Her husband standing close by said; "She didn't give me a bit of credit".

Ruthalie worked as director of released time Christian Education in Los Angeles county for many years. She became listed in WHO'S WHO of AMERICAN WOMEN. One of the greatest test of Christian Faith occurred when her oldest son James Terrel Heffner was shot by a drunken man. The murderer in prison was visited by the Pastor of the church where James had been a member. The Pastor succeeded in winning the man to a faith in Christ. The murderer was let off easy, spending only a year in prison. One year later when Ruthalie and her husband LeRoy, went back to Tennessee to clear up their sons estate, they attended the church their son attended.   There in the congregation was the converted murderer.   She underwent the ultimate trial of faith to forgive those who trespass against us.

The Heffners are now perennials who keep blooming and giving out in a long life. They have been strong leaders in Life for India mission, and in local church life. David, the remaining son is a supervisor in an airplane factory in Georgia.   You remember the daughter that the Doctor got thanked profusely for years earlier? That's Margaret; with her husband, Tom Brown. have pastored several churches. Their son, Clinton, made the headlines in the Show Low Arizona fire in 2002.   His wedding date occurred while he and his father were fighting the fire. On the date and at the time appointed, the fire men had the wedding at the fire station with fireman preacher Tom Brown tying the knot. Right afterward they all went back to fighting the fire.

When Sissy made Who's Who of American Women, I first thought, "What did she do to deserve that honor." God rebuked me for even thinking it. When you so completely invest your life in others and pattern a Godly life that inspires so many people. How can you do better than that? That's **Sissy**.

The Boy With Greasy Finger Nails

The arrival of the first born son was an important time to Jesse Wayman who looked forward to building an empire on the prairies. Dean was not only a year younger than his sister, Ruthalie, but also not as quick in mental skills. I suppose part of this is that boys come into their skills later in teen years.

 There was a guiding hand in the combination of the genes that gave the girl strong caring and supportive talents. That same guiding hand was certainly apparent in the oldest son. He had a quick mechanical and practical mind that could master the changes that came to Life on the Prairies. Father was comfortable with horses, but was slow to catch on to motorized machines. When the big Case tractor with harvester-thresher came, Father let his son learn how to run it. He was only 12 years old.

Dean became the teacher of the rest of the boys as they came into teen years. He had a mechanical brain that could fix anything. He learned to overhaul the motors. He took charge of the harvesting with the combine and tractor. It was as if he was born with a Mechanical mindset so sorely needed all the years of his life.

He was big brother who drove the horse and buggy to Fairview school as Four younger brothers came of school age. The year that Dean started High School at Goltry, The family moved across the county line to the farm house that Jesse Wayman had purchased two years before. We forsook the horse and buggy and walked a half mile to catch the school bus. The bus was a rig with canvas side curtains and no heater. Any bus advantage was lost in the fact that now we must walk a half mile against the North Wind to catch it. The wind comes from the north a lot in the winter. Prairies provide no barrier between us and the North Pole. The wind chill factor was much lower than the temperature.

In the Twenties times were pretty good for the farmers. One of the ways boys had of making some pin money was trapping for fur animals. The fur season would start around Thanksgiving time. Dean began early to do some trapping for skunk, opossum and whatever. He was not old enough to have a gun. One day in a bait set for opossum, he caught a coyote. He had to get a neighbor to help with it because he had no gun. The coyote brought a handsome price paid in big silver dollars. Those silver dollars were so huge in our eyes. All of us became avid trappers after that.

It was a big day when one Christmas Dean was given a single shot Stevens 22 Cal. rifle. The depression brought on a great drop in prices for the furs, but then everything we bought was much cheaper The furs were our pin money all through the depression days. In my story of THE ENTERPRENEUR, I tell of how we little boys caught a skunk by the tail and brought him home. I invite you to read it if you can stand the smell.

In the fall of the year ducks came across our area flying south for the winter. Any pond of water enticed them to stop and rest a spell. We had a small pond below the barn that would fill up with fall rain. Then on a neighbors farm there was a larger pond that enticed Teal and Mallards to stop for a swim. Dean took what little money he could muster to buy a double barrel shotgun for duck hunting. He had some occasional success mainly on the bigger pond and sometimes on the pond below the barn on the home place.

One day we younger boys found a badly shot up wooden decoy that some one had discarded. We took it home and fixed it up somewhat and painted it to look like a Mallard duck. While brother Dean was gone to town one wet misty day we placed the decoy down on the pond below the barn to entice real ducks. Several hours we watched to no avail. When Dean came home we decided to have some fun anyway. We rushed out to the pick-up acting excited as a hound dog chasing a rabbit. "Dean, there's a Mallard duck down on the pond."

Dean was always game for a duck dinner..   He grabbed the shotgun and loaded both barrels. Duck hunters know that you got to stay out of sight. Dean went far down the pasture away from the pond and crawled on his hand and knees up the canyon bed below the dam. The dam was not very high and he almost had to eat mud all the way to stay out of sight. His clothes got muddy from collar to cuff. His shoes and hair were caked with red clay, He reached the dam. He quickly peeked over the dam with the gun at ready. He saw the decoy and blasted it to smithereens with both barrels before he realized that he'd been had.

When Dean graduated from Goltry High School in 1933 the depression had deepened. The dust bowl days were at their worst. He was so vital to the operation of the farm that his only option was to work harder and longer hours. There was no prospect of college. No work was available as every city had long bread lines already. He was needed at home so badly; why look further? When the big threshing crew was started, Dean's Mechanical skill kept the big threshing machine going. There is no doubt father would have been helpless in the harvest season with out Dean. He served the family as Sissy had done after high school, without benefit to himself.

Dean was an inveterate teaser. He could lay it on thick and delighted in the verbal abuse he rendered. Back in high school days when he was a freshman and Ruthalie was a senior he tormented her about a gentleman in the Sr. Class whose last name was Becker. She had expressed some liking of him and

Dean's favorite torment was "Why don't you marry that Becker, and get it over with." It is immaterial that Mr. Becker never expressed any interest in Ruthalie. She was only fifteen her senior year.

Now it so happened that a few years later an unrelated Becker family rented the farm across the road from our farm. Our house and their house were a half mile apart. Barney Becker had a teen aged daughter named Violet. One summer Violet was the hired girl to help mother with the enormous task of feeding the threshing crews.

When Dean turned twenty-three, he worked up courage to ask father for the car on Saturday nights. He said he was going to Enid to a Movie. This went on for quite some months. He never spoke of having a girl friend so we had no idea what he was up to. Our curiosity was plaguing all of us. The fact that Dean had teased his sister so mercilessly set him up for what happened next.

One Saturday evening, One of we boys climbed up on the windmill tower to scout out where he went. He drove south a ways toward Enid. Then the scout reported him cutting back the other direction. A mile away the road ran north again and then back east this put him on the road a half mile north. All the boys turned that direction and sure enough the car was visibly driving into the Becker's home just a half mile away. The jig was up. We greeted Dean the next morning, "Why don't you marry that Becker and get it over with." He did.

He started married life on our old house where most of the family was born. It had only occasionally been occupied for the last eight years. With a few cows and a pick up truck he continued to work on the family farm and rented his own land. Dean was the only one of the twelve children that did not get a college education. With practical skills and hard work he accumulated farm after farm. Thirty years later he was worth more than all the rest of us combined.

His son and grandsons helped him with the farm work in later years. His two daughters became school teachers. Dean always was a part of the entire farm life at home as well as the vast acreage he accumulated on his own. He served on the school board. As an adult he made a commitment of his life to Christ. He served as an elder at the Liberty Church that had profoundly influenced the entire family for three generations.

Some interesting events that marked his life were the way he could overcome loss. One harvest he and a brother, Clarence, were harvesting wheat on the east place. At noon time they parked the rigs on the high hill in the adjacent pasture while they drove to his house for dinner. Evidently the wind whipped up while they were gone and sent the big harvester thresher rolling down the hill. It plunged into a deep canyon where it was impractical to remove. Dean notified neighbors with the same type of rigs that his combine was available to "Parts out". Farmers living so far from city could find an available replacement for broken parts of their machines close at hand.

Twenty years ago when I started researching for this story I made the comment about Dean. "I never remember Dean not having grease under his finger nails." I allowed Dean who was still living at that time to read what I was saying about him. He came to that part about the greasy nails. I saw him glance down at his finger nails, and sure enough, there was black grease under his nails. I'm sure there were times when his hands and nails were clean. I only remembered him as endlessly working, fixing, welding, repairing and greasing machinery. After all, grease is cheaper than machinery.

Dean came the closest to fulfilling fathers dream of an empire. He had many farms and the price of land escalated in the late seventies and early eighties. With the long lines at gasoline pumps in the seventies there was a great boost in oil search on the farms. Bonus prices for drilling rights brought prospects of making it big. You will remember the OPEC countries ploy to over produce drove many oil companies out of business. At this time years of bad weather plagued farms in that part of the country again, Interest rates were high and land prices had risen so that the cost of production was too much for the price of wheat. The government tried to offset low prices by paying farmers not to raise wheat.

Cattle were a good price. Wheat farmers could graze off the wheat and get paid for not harvesting. Selling the fattened cattle could beat the system. Dean went into big time cattle business. He prospered in spite of the uncertainties of the oil market and poor wheat prices.

If anyone makes money, the others jump in to get a chunk of it. By mid-eighties the prices of thin stock cattle were driven high by demand. Farmers sought to get paid for not harvesting their wheat. They needed thin stock to graze off the wheat before harvest to qualify for government money.

Like the crash of '29 when Jesse Wayman nearly lost it all, so Dean traveled the same road. He bought 500 head of thin stock cattle for spring grazing. The price was way beyond reason. He had to borrow big money to win the bid. Interest rates were in double digits. Bankers would lend him any amount he needed. His credit was perfect.

The Stock was shipped in from afar. Vaccinated and branded, the costs kept climbing. He trucked the stock to the grazing land.

Dean had a heart Attack; Dead at seventy-one.
As if death triggered the livestock prices, the bottom dropped out. The hole was deep.

The year ended, no market for fat steers. Land prices deteriorated. No one wants farms at a time when no one makes money.

His empire crashed like- his father's before him.

The vastness of American production and the hungry multitudes of the world have never found a way to wed. The dreams of empire died with him. He filled an enormous space in life and left a vast vacuum when he was gone.

The Wayman Brothers

 They were as unlike each other as brothers can be, but circumstances put them together for most of life.

James Elton was the third member of the Wayman family. Sixteen month later Clarence Kendall was born. Leadership in the family was already established in Ruthalie and Dean. James was easy to get along with and peaceable. He took life as it came and adapted himself into a supportive role as a follower. He called little attention to himself, but tried to let others excel.

Clarence moved as a maverick among us. He was close in age to James. His babyhood was shortened when another brother came along the following year. He was thrust into a middle child syndrome. His temperament needed something to be a leader in, but he was too late. He obtained attention by involving himself with everyone else in misdemeanors. As he grew older he was able to channel his leadership ability in a constructive manner.

When James was in the fourth grade at Fairview School, he had a sickly year with flu and colds that required a trip to the Doctors office to remove the tonsils. It was a botched job and he was sick a long time. Finally the Doctor came out to the ranch house. Mama and Papa held James in a chair while the doctor finished the tonsillectomy without anesthetic. I can remember as a five year old watching the process and the torture of my brother. I know it must have hurt the folks to have to hold him during the procedure. James missed so much school that year; he had to take the fourth grade twice. This put him and Clarence in the same grade all through the rest of grade school and High School.

James loved the 4-H Club and was a strong supporter of the younger boys in that activity. Clarence never joined 4-H Club but supported all of us who did and seemed to delight in our progress. Upon graduation from Goltry High School, there seemed no future for the boys. Ruthalie and LeRoy lived in Edmonds after their marriage where Central Teachers College was located. She invited the boys one at a time to live in their home and attend college.

An insight into their different personalities came through. Ruthalie said that James went out and socialized a lot but Clarence never did. They both became a part of their sisters Baptist church while there with her. Their help was needed so much in farm work that they could only get intermittent college first at Central and then at Okla. A& M in Stillwater.

It was in 1935 that James went in with a younger brother in the hog business. Clarence became involved but not wholeheartedly at first; later both became involved.

James was twenty-three and Clarence was twenty-two when their break came. It was cloaked in a dastardly deed of terrorism on Dec. 7, 1941. PEARL HARBOR BOMBING. It might as well have occurred in the living room of Jesse Wayman's farmhouse. Jesse Wayman had four single young men out of high school in choice physical health and expert with a rifle. James and Clarence both enlisted immediately into the Navy. Both found service in the Pacific. Byron joined the navy a few months later and then Phil joined the army in Sept 1942.

There were two national calamities that shaped the family immensely. The first one was the Great Depression. The second was World War II. Both of them frustrated the empire that Jesse Wayman envisioned for his family. Both of them disciplined the family for something greater that God had in mind. Jesse Wayman had good intentions, but Uncle Sam is greater than my father.

There was a more powerful force at work than either Uncle Sam or Jesse Wayman. Mother had a strong faith that God was Almighty and more powerful than Germany or Japan or Uncle Sam. She pursued prayer like a prospector who had found a nugget and knew there was more like it in the gold mine.

I repeat this incident because it was the force that held the family together when the boys scattered on the land and sea. Mother took her well-worn Bible as each boy went away and read the 9lst Psalm. She claimed those promises for each of them as they left home.

He that dwells in the secret place of the most High shall abide under the shadow of the Almighty. I will say of the Lord, he is my refuge and my fortress; my God; in Him will I trust. Surely He will deliver thee from the snare of the fowler and from the noisome pestilence. He shall cover thee with his feathers, and under his wings shalt thou trust. His Truth shall be thy shield and buckler. Thou shalt not be afraid for the terror by night; nor for the arrow that flies by day; nor for the pestilence that walks in darkness; nor for the destruction that wastes at noon day. A thousand shall fall at thy side and ten thousand at thy right hand. but it shall not come nigh thee.

We went through Sea battles, Land battles and Air attacks as well as dangers in jungle warfare and all came home. Other mothers prayed for their sons who did not return. Asking WHY is a futile question. I know it worked for us.

James and Clarence both came home from the war. With the GI educational benefit they both graduated from Oklahoma A&M College.

They both returned to the farm and developed the purebred hog business. They became known across the Midwest as the WAYMAN BROTHERS. They became famous for champions. James taught Agriculture and worked with the Future Farmers of America.

A lovely young lady in Helena barely out of high school finally caught James' eye. He married Donna Wadkins. He was thirty one years of age.

They bought the Constant place that Jesse Wayman had rented for many years. Donna became the rural mail carrier. Her route was mostly on red clay dirt roads. Through rain, snow, cold and heat the mail had to go every day. She still maintained the farm after James died at eighty. He is buried at the Karoma cemetery.

Clarence, the one who was involved with others, returned to the home place. He and James both received high honors as **Farmer of the Year** in the state of Okla. Clarence worked with Fair Boards and with 4-H Clubs and FFA Clubs. He was an expert in hog judging. He helped with the various farms that Dean and James had and farmed the home place for the folks while they lived.

He was so involved with every one and with every thing that went on in the community that he never took time to find a wife. An amazing story unfolded as he was in his sixties. Let me explain.

Sister Ruthalie and husband, LeRoy were very active in a Baptist church in Sunland, California. They were deeply involved in this church since moving west before WWII. In 1982 the church hired a little retired school teacher as organist for the church services. At a church social one evening Ruthalie engaged the new organist in delightful conversation. Ruthalie found out that the lady was a school teacher originally from Oklahoma.

Ruthalie asked her where she taught in Oklahoma. The little lady smiled brightly and said, "You wouldn't have heard about it, it was a little town in northwest Oklahoma."

"I came from that area," said Ruthalie, "What was the name of the town?"

"Goltry" she said.

Ruthalie fairly screamed, "I graduated from Goltry high school in 1930. What year were you there?"

The little lady smiled again, "I taught High school English there just one year in 1936-37".

Ruthalie could hardly contain herself. "You would have some of my brothers in high school at that time." Do you remember having Wayman boys in your classes?"

"Why yes," she said, "two of them were in my senior English class that year and I believe there were more in lower English classes".

"That would be James and Clarence who graduated in 1937 from Goltry high school, and Byron would have been a junior and Phil a freshman that year."

The lady's name was Trudy Berry. She was first year out of college when she taught at Goltry. Ruthalie found out that Trudy had married, & had one son. She had lost her husband a few years ago. Ruthalie told her about all the Wayman boys that Trudy had taught high school English to.

Trudy perked up her ears when she heard that Clarence had graduated from the same college she did, and especially that he had never married. Trudy was interested in this bachelor man that she remembered in Goltry high school so long ago.

A few months later Ruthalie and LeRoy celebrated their 50th wedding anniversary at Sunland, California. Many of Ruthalie's brothers and sisters came out for the celebration. Clarence also came. He had been in Ruthalie's home many times when he was stationed at San Diego in the war.

Trudy found opportunity to renew acquaintance with him. She found a figurine of a mama pig nursing piglets and gave it to Clarence. It did the trick.

When he returned to Oklahoma a correspondence occurred. It resulted in Clarence's first marriage to The lady that many of we boys knew as Miss Berry. She came back to Oklahoma and lived at the little house Clarence had built on the home place. Trudy opened Clarence world to travel and finer things. His world became larger and he loved it and little Miss Trudy. She was so petite and still a pretty lady, no matter her age.

Clarence was the last of the nine boys that married. Most of us were grand parents. He also was the first of the boys to lose his partner. Trudy died with cancer in five years. Clarence was single again. Trudy had a friend in San Diego whom she had worked with in college teaching. This friend, Ruby, had also lost her husband. The two ladies had been fast friends for years.

When Trudy knew she was dying, she brought her friend Ruby out to the ranch to introduce her to Clarence. Clarence had taken so many years finding his first wife, Trudy did not want him to resort back to another long lonely life. She fixed the plan for the future.

A Few months after Trudy died, Clarence and Ruby were married. She had a large beautiful home in San Diego where Clarence retired to and spent many years with Ruby and her Mother, called "Mama C." Both "Mama C" and Ruby thought Clarence was the best in the world and told him so.

Every good thing comes to an end if it's on earth. "Mama C" passed away ten years later. Ruby also died with cancer the next year. Clarence moved again back to the town of Goltry and spends his retirement years close to the farm and the hogs that he likes to raise and show.

James and Clarence were the **Wayman Brothers**, so different and yet so much alike. Their lives intertwined so much. They both served their nation well. They both served their own community. They both made large strides in the purebred hog business; they both excelled in farm life. Both filled a large space as good, honest men.

The Entrepreneur

The fifth child of the Tribe of Jesse was named Byron Lee. He was born late in the year that caused him to start school while still five years of age. He found it difficult to keep up in school. He was awkward at play and caught lots of scuff from others who were more agile. He was tone deaf. He could not carry a tune. He felt rejected in activities with others because of his handicaps. The family nick-named him Barney.

There was an awkward, backward character in the comic strips at that time called Barney Google. The kids in school called Byron, Barney-Google. for short. He accepted the humiliation because in his own mind it fit him.

Number six in the Tribe of Jesse was Philip Earl (that's me). I tried to be number one, but was born too late. My ambition was to get ahead of the one ahead of me. I hassled with Byron a lot and blamed him for the mishaps.

One day mother asked us to watch over The baby who was two years younger than I. We were assigned to see that he went to sleep on the bed without falling off first. It was boring work. I began to wrestle with Barney on the bed. The baby fell off between the bed and wall and hung there muffling his cry. I ran into the kitchen to tell Mother. "I never, Barney did." Barney had to defend himself, "I never, Phil did!" By the time mother deciphered what it was that one or the other or both had done, the baby was blue with suffocation. Fortunately mother got there in time to rescue the baby without damage. "I think!"

Another time we were inside on a stormy day and we were bored with it. We started racing from one end of the house to the other and stopping with our hands on the window glass in the Living room. It was fun to beat Barney and I hit that glass so hard it broke. You can imagine my frantic cry to mother, "I never, Barney did". Byron of course was of a different persuasion, "I never, Phil Did." Finding the blame doesn't fix any broken window. It had to be boarded up until papa could get some glass in town and fix it. Needless to say, we never did that again.

Because of closeness in age we did a lot of things together. We were as different as brothers can be. I liked to do things with Barney. He was kind, honest and unselfish and easy to take advantage of. This fed my ego. Byron and I often stayed at grandfather Secord's place in summer time when we were too young to be much help. One day grandpa brought home some cantaloupe that was so good at lunch-time. I noted that there were a lot of them in the root cellar.

Along in mid-afternoon the thought of those juicy cool cantaloupes gave me fits in my mind. I begged grandma if Barney and I could have a cantaloupe. After making a nuisance of myself enough, grandma consented. I went down in the root cellar and got a nice cantaloupe. I went out side and called Barney to come.

Barney didn't respond right away. I took a knife out of the kitchen drawer and cut the cantaloupe in half (or at least in two pieces). It was obvious that one piece was bigger than the other. I had been trained when at home that you treat everyone fairly and think of others first. I pondered the situation. I came to the conclusion that if Byron was here, he would divide the melon and give me the biggest piece because he was such a kind unselfish brother. Since he would give me the biggest piece and I would want the biggest piece, I saved him the trouble of having to make a decision. I took the biggest piece and ate it.

I kept calling Barney but he delayed in coming. I had no sooner finished my piece and thrown the rind in the garbage when Barney came in. "Grandma gave us permission to eat this cantaloupe" I told him. Byron looked at the piece on the counter and with grateful attitude he proceeded to cut it exactly in half. Now I knew my brother was a kind, generous boy, not like me. I did not see any reason to spoil his generosity by telling him what I had done. We shared together in the other piece and thanked grandma for her kindness.

Later in life I had to bare my conscience with Byron about my deceit. But he didn't remember the incident and readily forgave me. There were unusual qualities in Byron that through the years I learned to respect highly. He was so much better boy than I was. I appreciated him a whole lot.

Bring `Em Back Alive

In the midst of the depression a skunk fur would bring a dollar. Now that was a lot of money considering that a mans wage in winter time was a dollar a day. That's where that saying came from - **Another day, another dollar**. Byron was a thinker upper. He suggested to me "Let's go Skunk Hunting!" You can count on me to go for an adventure like that. Six year old brother Hugh tagged along with us. We were not old enough to carry a gun or anything dangerous.

There were several deep canyons on the ranch and we scoured the closest one for a Skunk Den. There under a ledge of rock was a hole that was big enough for a skunk. It ran back in the bank so that you could not see the end. It looked promising even to our inexperienced eyes. "How are we going to get him to come out?" Byron had the answer. "Phil, go up on the fence and get a section of barbed wire and we'll twist him out of there." I ran up a fourth mile to the fence row. I had no tool to cut the wire so I looked for a place where there was a splice. I unwired the splice and then back ten feet or so I bent the wire back and forth until it broke. I hoped the cows wouldn't find the hole in the fence until we returned the barbed wire. What happened next made us forget to return the wire.

We made a V in one end of the wire and L shaped the twisting end. We started it in the hole and by twisting and pushing the wire went in out of sight. All of a sudden it began to tighten and we could smell the acrid smell of a skunk. We knew we had one on the wire. All three of us began to pull and p-u-l-l until here came a black and white striped real skunk out of the hole. Of course his tail is what was entangled in the wire. He came out with the dangerous end already for action. It was like we had a Devil by the tail, and didn't know what to do with him.

We dropped the wire lest we get **skunk-on** while we consulted what to do next. The poor scared creature untangled himself from the wire. He wasn't about to go back in the hole and suffer that indignity again.

The skunk headed up the hill toward our ranch house. We thought we could just herd him home. When the skunk sensed that we wanted him to go that direction, he changed his mind and headed the wrong direction. Now us **"Bring em back Alivers"** had not done enough homework before engaging in battle. We had to learn by experience.

Unfortunately a boy can outrun a skunk. I thought if I could just throw my coat around him and pick him up in my arms, I would not get any **skunk-on** me.

I tried that ploy. It worked for a half minute. The skunk wormed out of the coat and resumed his race toward the ranch house again. We were less than a quarter mile from the house when the skunk found another shallow hole in the bank and slipped in.

After a brief executive meeting on what-to-do-now, Barney came up with this great idea. He said, "I have heard that if you grab his tail and hold his head down, he can't get anything on you."

I readily agreed because I had no better idea. "Yeah, why don't **you** try that"? My brave brother, Barney, reached into that hole where that live skunk was and grabbed his tail and pulled him out of there.

"Come on boys, Let's go Home." he said.

All of us were grinning like chimpanzees as we walked into the farmyard with our trove. Papa saw us coming, and he began to holler in exasperation. Mama smelled us coming and she began to scream. The boys were somehow not as enthusiastic as we thought they would be. Some one thought of putting the skunk in a barrel until a proper method of disposal was achieved.

What happened next is fortunately muted in memory. We were so **skunked-up** that we had ceased to smell it ourselves. You can bury clothes and take care of the skunk smell in the cloth; but there's a law against leaving boys in the clothes when you do that.

Barney's first effort at making money ended in a mess. Oh well, we just chalk it up to experience. We never did it that way again. There is a sequel to this story at the close of this chapter on Byron's life.

In the summer of 1934 Byron and I were given an opportunity by Riley Constant to stay at his farmhouse while he and his wife vacationed. We would milk cows and care for chickens and spend the night at the house. We did chores again in the morning before coming home for breakfast next day.

We were pleased with opportunity to have cream & eggs to sell. It was always a delight to have a nice screened summer porch for a bedroom to ourselves for two months. When Mr. & Mrs. Constant came home we resumed farm living as usual at home thinking we were adequately paid for our endeavor.

A few days later Mr. and Mrs. Constant came driving into our place. They called Byron and me out to their car. They asked Byron to hold out his hand. Mr. Constant took out a wad of freshly printed $1 bills. He counted into Byron's hand thirty of those bills. Then he called me over. He counted thirty new bills into my trembling hand. We were so overwhelmed that we kept trying to pull back, but he would not be deterred until we each had the full reward for our summer activity.

What a blessing these neighbors were to our family. We swam in their pond. We hunted on their land.

Father rented a hundred acres of their wheat land. After they were both gone, my brother James bought the farm and lived there.

I took my money and bought purebred Poland China gilt from Turney Bossart at Kremlin. My father had done business with Turney earlier in life. This bred sow became the foundation of the hog business that limped along in the depression years. Younger brothers kept it going in the war years and then James and Clarence made the herd famous as Wayman Brothers after WWII.

Byron on the other hand acted on his own. He went into the turkey business. Turkeys thrived on the grasshoppers that plagued the prairie country in those years. He had quite a flock of turkeys and always managed to make some money in the turkey business.

Byron graduated in 1938 from Goltry high. By special arrangements with Riley Constant, Byron went into broiler business. Mr. Constant had a beautiful chicken house with three compartments that he was no longer using. Byron put everything he had accumulated into this enterprise.

He finally had all three compartments full in three stages of development. He would sell the fat broilers and replace them with starter chicks. The previous starters would now be feathered and moved into the fattening section. His success seemed assured. One of the compartments housing the new chicks required kerosene brooder equipment.

One Friday night in the fall the family all attended a Farmers Union meeting in Goltry. On the way home we saw on the horizon a glow that indicated fire. As we topped the rise going to the Constant place we saw the entire chicken house ablaze. It not only destroyed all his broilers but also the beautiful chicken house that he was using. All he had worked for was gone and he was in debt to rebuild the building that he was using. He had no insurance. I suppose by modern standards he didn't lose much, but he lost all he had. That's tough by any standard.

At a revival meeting in Liberty church Byron turned his life over to God. His steadfast faith never wavered for he found purpose and meaning for his life.

At that time the Air Force was building the Enid airfield for training pilots. Byron got a job as a carpenter's helper. He rode to work with a neighbor, Don White, who also worked in Enid. With his money, Byron rebuilt the chicken houses that had burned down.

When the infamous act at Pearl Harbor occurred, Byron was 21 and eligible for immediate draft. He joined the Navy. He became a sea cook. He spent many months right at Norman Oklahoma. He finally had duty in the Pacific on Admiralty islands.

Somewhere along the line he felt the call to the ministry while in the Navy. He worked with Men who had been hurt in the war. He became Chaplains helper while doing his work as sea cook. His testimony of his encounters with these men at war was printed up in the Free Methodist magazine.

A pretty nurse at Deaconess Hospital in Oklahoma City had a pen friendship going during the war. When Byron came home He married the lady, Ramona Andis.

While working at various types of business: Byron achieved a master's degree in sociology. He was Pastor of several Free Methodist churches in Oklahoma. He taught college classes at SW Missouri in Joplin and at SW Teachers college in Lawton, Okla. He built several houses. He was a great camp cook for large groups.

It was while Byron was teaching at SW Missouri College that the sequel to **Bring 'em back Alive** occurred.

In my own constant traveling from the West Coast back to denominational headquarters I was privileged to visit Byron many times. I stopped by Joplin in midweek when Byron was teaching a night class in

Sociology. He was working on the Depression Work
Ethic.

He came up with this idea that I could tell one of my
stories that fit that era of time as a guest lecturer
that evening. I was pleased with the opportunity.

To the delight of the students and the consternation
of Professor Wayman, I chose to tell the story of the
skunk hunt. I told about brave brother Barney
pulling this skunk out by the tail and carrying him
home alive to make a dollar.

Just at that moment in my story, an acrid odor
seeped through an open window of the class room. It
so punctuated the story that the student's thought
they must be imagining it. Evidently a real live
skunk was listening in and thought my story **stunk**.
You be the judge but both Byron and I along with
thirty college students can verify the accuracy of the
sequel to the story of **Bring em back Alive.**

He and Ramona raised three children, Ruth, Ron, &
Neil. His life exemplified the grace, kindness and
patience of a Christian gentleman. When our parents
were dead Byron took his inheritance in the farm at
Glencoe. He was in cattle business while pastoring at
Stillwater.

Byron was an entrepreneur. He could figure out a
way to make a living where ever he was. He moved
from assignment to assignment, did a project and

moved on before he could enjoy the fruit of his labor. Barney was like Barnabas in the Bible who was called a **'Brother**.' He was one of the humblest men I ever met. He never was bitter or complaining but served patiently. It was while pastoring at the church in Stillwater that he built a large pond on his property in Glencoe. He had in mind to build a house there to retire in. Again his plans were thwarted.

Byron took a **short-cut** to his final assignment at the age of sixty-one. With the sure hope that he had of eternal life in Christ, he will now have plenty time and space to finish and enjoy any project that needs done.

Copy-Cat, Mama's Pet, & Squeaky Backbone

I'm Philip Earl. I was named after my dad whose middle name was Earl. Also one of mother's brothers was called Earl. If I saw something done I would copy it or else. I envied what someone else succeeded at and tried to do the same. That was what we called a copy-cat in school.. Without natural talent my efforts were trial and error. I told about my escapades with Byron who was just older. If I did not succeed I would blame Byron for the failure.

I rode the buggy to Fairview School for my first grade. There was only one other in the first grade. Her name was Velma White. I suffered much humiliation that year because I was the smallest boy in the school of eight grades. I was last picked for games. I was called names for making the outs in the ball game. I also was called a name unfit for polite company because I could not make it to the outhouse on time.

The school clothing for little boys was union-alls. They were one-piece garment instead of a shirt and pants. There was a row of buttons in the rear that were difficult for a little boy to manipulate. This caused a crisis. By the time you got them unbuttoned it was too late. Then when you tried to button them up again the buttons were always behind you no matter how fast you turned around.

When the day got boring, big boys found delight in sharpening their pencil often. Since the sharpener was at a distance from their seats the boys would come by the first grade area on the way to the sharpener. While I was busy studying, they would reach behind me and pull on the flap that came unbuttoned too easily when they did it. I would be the staring stock of a room full of kids while I tried to get them buttoned again in some order. By that time the pencil had been sharpened and the big boy came by my row again and pulled on the flap again. It was worth the scolding of the teacher to see my face red and my fumbling hands working on the buttons where you can't see. Several of those big guys were bigger than the teacher so what could she do.

I found myself in other real embarrassing situations because I tried to do what I'd seen others do. If some one said I couldn't do it that was like sic 'em to a hound dog. Older boys at school tested me to see how tough I was. They would twist my arms or pinch or hit me but I would not cry. It wasn't the code to be a sissy.

In spite of the annoyance, I was the smartest boy in my class. I was the only boy in my class. My first grade was my greatest lesson in life and I treasure it today. I watched the fourth graders doing ciphering in front of the room. I spent my time watching and copying them instead of my own work; the same with spelling or anything that went on in the one room schoolhouse. I found school fairly easy after that.

Some big neighbor boys would come occasionally to the farm to play. They liked to pair up the younger boys to watch us fight. I was always paired with Byron. In the ensuing scuffle, Byron would begin to cry. I interpreted this to mean that I was built for power.

There was a big kid down at the school that aggravated me and I took him on. I thought if I could whip my older brother, I could whip anyone my own age. I found myself on the bottom of a fight that I could not escape from. I made lots of mistakes but I learned awfully fast. I found I was not built for power. I was built for speed. That way I managed to discover what my talents were not and adjusted accordingly.

The Seventh child in the family was born on Feb 29th, 1924, which was leap year. His birth date only occurs every four years. Hugh DeLynn did not try to keep up with his older brothers like I did. He reverted to being a mama boy. If he were hurt or even close to hurt, he would run and tell mama.

I told of that incident where Byron and I knocked him off the bed and mama rescued him from suffocation. After that he would cry and hold his breath to get mama's attention. I remember a time when I was rocking in the chair that I rocked into Hugh. He cried like I was killing him and held his breath until he went unconscious. I was so scared thinking I had killed my little brother. Mama had caught on to his ploy by that time and laid him out to sleep. He woke up a few hours later. He was all right, I guess.

When Hugh was two, he got a kiddy tricycle for Christmas. I liked this toy and took it whenever I could and rode it. Hugh was too small to contest, he would just go and tell mama. I was too big for it. I broke it down on several occasions. This raised the disgust of father who had to cobble it up again.

Hugh was small and a cute little guy. He was the favorite of aunts and uncles to whom he clung for his recognition. When Hugh stayed at grandpa Secord's house, he was the favorite of uncle Ted and aunt Opal. They were still at home as young adults. Ted was a teaser who liked to tease Hugh. They nicknamed him "Hootsy" for short.

Hugh would get excited when talking. His mind was quicker than his tongue so he did not sound out his R. Uncle Ted delighted in mimicking what Hootsy said. Hugh talked about "the boid that had a nest in the twee with thwee eggs in it that now had none". Ted called him a "Boid egg sucko that sucked the boid eggs that's why there weren't any more." Hugh said "I dwank fwee glasses of wato but I do not remember when." Ted picked up on this and reported "Hootsy dwank fwee gwasses of wato but he does not wemembo whetho it was befoe dinno or afto, but I fink it was immediately befo suppo." Hugh seemed to enjoy the ribbing and was a happy boy.

Though all three girls in the family graduated either 1st or 2nd in their class, Hugh was the only one of the nine boys to graduate at the top. The war was on when he graduated from High School. The draft age lowered that year to eighteen. Hugh and I both registered for the draft at the same time. I had just turned twenty. I was immediately put in I-A.

Hugh had time to go to A&M College at Stillwater that fall. He took ROTC training that kept him out of the draft. He developed a hernia and was given a lower draft classification. While at the college, he attended the Free Methodist church. He experienced a heart warming and life changing encounter with God that made him change directions toward the ministry.

The following year he took a year in Central College at McPherson, Kansas. With summer school he was able to graduate from Greenville, Illinois College in one more year. While older brothers were at war, Hugh was the first of the boys to graduate from college. He graduated from Asbury Seminary two years later.

Hugh never looked back except to marry a childhood acquaintance. When he came home from seminary, he was surprised to see the daughter of family friends had blossomed into a beautiful young lady. He determined in his resolute way, "That's the girl I'm going to marry". He never asked Betty Shields for her opinion in the matter. I assume she must have been willing because it happened right away.

His unwavering faith in God made him a great blessing to many people. Any task he started, he held on like a bulldog to see it through. He pioneered and built a church in Midwest City. He became a skilled jack-of-all-trades. He built many churches. He made a success of everything he set out to do. He was made superintendent of the Free Methodist churches of Oklahoma. He was guiding hand on the board at Deaconess Hospital. He was always building or fixing up something including the Perkins camp ground. He was a livestock and wheat farmer, and an avid fisherman.

He and Betty raised five children. All three boys have doctorates and are in ministry relationships. The girls are teachers. In retiring years his keen mind has conceived of a sun-powered automatic cattle feeder that he has patented and sells.

Now that I have the advantage of long distance hindsight, I am amazed that my helpless little brother became a powerful influence on so many people. The boys saw everything fixed with baling wire on the ranch. It's amazing how all us became involved in building houses and churches and pioneering various enterprises. It goes to show that **"You can't tell by the looks of a frog how far he can jump"**.

Robert Eugene was the eighth child of the Tribe of Jesse. He did not seem to excel at anything while growing up. He seemed lost in the shuffle. He clung for security to older brothers. He learned what he knew by listening carefully and trying to do that same thing. A slender frame thwarted his ability. He was not built for power or speed.

His talent was perception of the situation and making the most of it. He would watch others and follow suit. He called himself, **the smartest of the Wayman boys.** Being far down the line in pecking order he had adequate opportunity to **shut up and listen**. This way he could accumulate the combined wisdom of his older brothers.

Though his name is Robert, he was always "Bob" to us. Uncle Ted called him **Bobbity-Bob-Bob** for short. He found security in familiar things. Robert was nearly four when the family moved a half-mile to the west place farm. Mother, the girls and the furniture went by wagon. The boys all walked across the hill. As supper time approached, Bob anxiously looked up the path across the hill and said, "I want to go home."

He was so skinny he hardly left a shadow. It was not because he was underfed. He was like the runt of the litter figuring where he could get to the trough early or stay longer to catch up. Always hungry, he would get as fretful as a hungry hog at feeding time. He coined the phrase. **"My stomach is rubbing against my back bone."**

One day Bob made his usual early appearance for dinner and was greeted with the tantalizing smell of fresh baked cake. One of the ladies was making frosting for the freshly baked cake. He used his usual lead-in about his stomach rubbing against his backbone. The Lady was just creaming the shortening to make white frosting. She responded, "Here, this will grease your stomach to keep it from wearing through". She gave him a heaping spoonful of the creamed shortening. He voraciously put the whole thing in his mouth without tasting it. The icky stuff nearly turned him inside out. He choked while trying to find a place to honorably dispose of the stuff. He never used that phrase again, but he still was always hungry with his backbone squeaking.

In a large family the smaller ones were at the foot of the table where food comes last. Chickens were cut in as many pieces as possible to feed many people. Even with two chickens a meal, the smaller boys would be left with inferior pieces. As they grew bigger the timid wised up and tried different ploys to achieve a meatier piece.

Because Bob was himself was far down in the pecking order, he became good at cajoling the two younger brothers who came along many years later. He would holler out, "Save me the neck; Don't anybody take the neck." The younger ones, if they got to the platter before Bob, would grab that preferred piece that Bob was asking for. They put one over on Bob and showed that they were Smart Wayman boys also.

I remember when Bob got so sick. He had summer flu of some kind. We had cantaloupe for dinner and so mother took in the half cantaloupe so Bob could have some in bed. He looked up and his eyes got big, "Is that all for me." He had barely eaten it when he went into a spasm; retching and vomiting that scared the whole family. Father called the doctor, who came out four miles on dirt roads to our house. When they told him what happened, he laughed, and went to help the boy.

I stood by with mixed emotions. I was angry to think the doctor could laugh when my brother was dying. On the other hand this kind of thing was routine for country doctors. To think he would respond day or night to the needs of even my little brother and drive out to minister to him. I am now awed by it.

In the chapter on Liberty Church I tell what moved Bob to accept Christ. He liked to go to church because he and his peers played games outside. He was a friendly boy and had lots of friends. When his brother Phil went forward in church to get saved; Bob was startled. He thought, "Why would Phil need to do that? He is as good a boy as I am." Bob finally calculated that if his brother needed to get saved, it was good to do the same thing. Since he was always trying to follow his brothers in any good thing, he showed that he just might be the **smartest of the Wayman boys.**

Bob was in high school during WWII and he took hold of all the things the older brothers had been doing. He excelled in 4-H Club. He took the purebred hog business to grand champion status at the State Fair. Uncle Ted labeled him now as **"professor pork"**. He helped the folks during the war years to maintain the farm and avoided draft with farm deferment until the war ended.

When the rest of the boys came home, Bob went into the service and served in occupation Army in Japan. He rose rapidly in rank. He got into a good deal by volunteering to teach English to the many Japanese who wanted to learn our language. He used the Bible to teach English. This set him up for his life calling.

He came home and renewed his work at Okla. State U. at Stillwater. He became associated with the Southern Baptist church in Stillwater. He felt the call to preach and went to the Golden Gate seminary. He rejoined the army reserves as a chaplain and served many years in part time duty. He retired as a Lt. Colonel.

He pioneered several churches and pastored others. "Oh yes", I almost forgot to mention that his **"Stomach rubbing against his backbone"** has long since been adequately cured.

After retirement from the military, he planted an orchard near Lancaster Calif., where he raises fruit to sell and eat.

The Story Of The Rings
(True Story from WWll)

Phil stopped at the jeweler's counter and his eyes moved along the shelf where the ring sets were carefully display in rich velour boxes. "May I help you?" a polite young man asked from behind the counter. Phil looked up through his tri-focals, fumbled inside his overcoat and pulled out an envelope. From it he extracted a badly worn set of rings. The diamond from the engagement ring was missing and the gold bands of both rings were worn badly to almost thread size. He handed the rings to the young man behind the counter:

"I need to replace these rings with a new set, you can see they are a bit worn." The Jeweler agreed that they about had it.

"Do you have anything that looks like these rings would have looked Thirty years ago?" Phil asked.
"Oh no," the young man smiled, "but I have lots of others that are in that quality range, Of course they are more expensive now than they were that long ago."

The Jeweler moved over and started pulling out set after set, commenting on the quality and beauty of each one. Phil hesitated. There was story in those old rings that made them worth far more than the beautiful new diamond and intricately designed wedding band. His mind raced back through the years, it was World War II.

There was this lovely Christian girl with red hair that he had met while serving in the Army in Oregon. For a few months they had enjoyed occasional company when orders came to move on. A timid letter back to her from California was answered with a sweet smelling letter in return and interest grew.

When orders came to ship out to the Pacific theater of war, Phil managed to get a week-end pass and traveled by bus back to Corvallis. He only had a few hours. She was so beautiful and gracious he could not leave without knowing what the prospects were. He popped the question. She surprised him with a ready "YES" The bus left so soon after to take him back to port of embarkation in California.

First to New Guinea, and then to the Philippine liberation in Luzon, the lonely soldier found comfort in dreaming of the day when. While on the front line one day a letter came already one month old. She mentioned in her cheerful way that "this young man who starting coming to the church has taken an interest in me."

It didn't sound cheerful to Phil, slogging it out in the heat and rain of the jungle and enduring the dangers of war, to realize that someone else might see in her the same qualities he did. The other fellow had the definite advantage of distance and availability at that time. I knew a boy at hand was worth two overseas.

Phil prayed about this matter and asked God to help him know what to do about it. He needed to give her a ring. "That's It a RING! but how?" God only knew how long it would be before he could return and take care of such things. The war and danger was ever present. He sat down that night by flickering candle light and penciled a letter to a pastor in Lompoc Calif. where he had attended church.   He asked the minister if he would be so kind as to look up a nice set of rings. "Let me know the price and I will send the money. Would you send it on to my girl for me?"

A long month went by with dangers and heat and enemy encounter. Phil was sent to the Panay and Negros Island invasions on a supply mission. A letter arrived one day post marked "Dallas, Texas".   No return address on it. His heart sank. He thought he had gotten a "Dear John" letter. He found a quiet place and with trembling hands opened the envelope to read: "Dearest Phil, Don't be upset. I'm on my way to Georgia with a girl friend and her husband.   I thought it would be an opportunity to see the country." "Whew." Phil sighed with relief and wiped the sweat off his brow.

Within a few days there came simultaneous letters from his sweetheart in Columbus, Georgia with a new address and from the minister in Lompoc.   The minister had already selected a set of rings and quoted the price. Phil wasted no time in sending a money order to the minister friend and gave him a little extra to send it to the address in Georgia. Then seven days later he wrote a letter to his sweetheart in Georgia. He explained his position and asked her to accept the tokens of his affection that would be coming momentarily.

Exactly two weeks later, in the morning mail, the letter arrived in Columbus, Georgia. Alma was excited as a girl winning the beauty contest. She rushed to share the news with her married girl friend. The ladies were both excitedly talking when the door bell rang and a Special Delivery package came for Miss Alma Wehmeir. She tore the package open. There were the rings that the letter promised were coming.

How could such timing have occurred in war time from half way around the world except by the oversight of a caring God. Phil was awed by the timing of it. He could never do it as perfectly himself

"Sir, is something wrong?" The clerk asked anxiously. The dreamy look disappeared from the eyes of the balding headed man standing by the jewelry case.

"Oh Excuse me," Phil explained, "I was reminiscing about the history of the old ring set."

He looked at the new ones being offered: "You know young man, now that my marriage has outlasted the rings, I suppose no new set could adequately tell what this lady means to me. there is a lot of living attached to the old ones."

Phil pointed to a lovely set of rings and paid the clerk. He thanked the patient jeweler and started to leave.

He turned back and said; "please pardon this sentimental old fellow. I've had a lovely Christian lady stick with me through difficult times and good times. She mothered three fine children. She was my best friend, my housekeeper, my wash lady, my cook and dishwasher, my nurse and traveling companion. She unselfishly lived her life to make me look good. We've shared joy and tough times together. We still love each other as we did at the start. Those rings sealed a successful happy marriage." The clerk smiled, "I agree."

A Girl That Came In The Nick Of Time

The prospect of a ninth child is not particularly a heraldic event. Seven boys in a row; Ruthalie had about given up hope of ever having a sister. The boys were not aware of the indignities that would lie ahead if the oldest sister ever left home. They however were in desperate struggle for status among so many boys. To the boys even a girl was better than another boy.

Complication required mother to go to the town where the Doctor's house was used as a hospital. Father took mother in the "Model T without a Top" in the early August morning. Sissy was left in charge. Dean had the new Case tractor out in the field plowing. James and Clarence were running teams of horses cultivating the row crop. The rest of the boys didn't know too much about what was going on.

It was chore time at night before father came driving home alone. He parked the Model T in the garage and went in the house to find his daughter. **"You have a baby sister"**. He announced. Sissy let out a whoop and rushed outside to tell the news to every living creature. **"I have a Baby Sister."**

That was different than any other message usually delivered on such occasions. Boys dropped what they were doing and came to the house to hear about this new thing called a "baby sister". Father was already in his overalls and going out to take charge of chores and had no time to celebrate.

Betty Lucille was named after an Aunt Lucille. We boys envisioned a dainty little helpless girl that would want to do house work, wash and dry dishes, and cook lots of good food that men and boys worked hard to provide. She should smile and be happy that she was privileged to have so many smarter brothers to tell her what to do. That's what it says in the Bible somewhere. I think it's in the book of Hezekiah. It's exasperating when a fellow can't find the chapter and verse.

The little sister was a take charge type of girl. She played the games boys played and competed with the boys. If there was anything boys could do, girls could do it better. We nicknamed her **Man Betty**. We lived in a chauvinistic age when women barely had gained the right to vote. Mama's name was not even on the title to the farm. The hog business became J.E. Wayman and sons. Daughters did not count in the economics of the day. Father even planned to give each boy a farm (160 Acres) but the girls would marry farmers. Let this old grandpa say: You've come a long ways Baby!.

It wasn't that Betty lacked one whit of being a lady, It was that we had a prejudiced mind-set that needed major adjustment. We had been schooled in a family of boys. We were sons of a father with high male ego. She was not only highly capable in many endeavors but had a brilliant mind as well. She asserted her intellect early before going to the first grade. She demanded books to read, an eagerness to learn, catch up and then excel all her siblings.

Betty was only five years old when big sister Ruthalie was married. We boys thought she should take over the kitchen like Ruthalie. Mama rescued her by forcing us older boys to take turns in the kitchen for a few years. I hated it. I learned to appreciate the work that women do. It didn't hurt us anywhere but our pride and that needed to hurt. We boys that took turns in the kitchen all have helped our partners in the housework in married life.

Within a few years Betty was the main kitchen help. She learned to sew, cook, and prepare any thing from the garden or the livestock. In those days father had a hammer mill that ground up grain for animal feed. By using a fine screen he also made whole wheat flour for baking and cereal. The same was done with corn that provided a good corn bread.

There were times when father took a load of wheat to the mill at pond Creek some thirty miles away and had it ground into flour. The flour for our family was in a fifty pound sack. The sack material was cotton. As a bonus the company would color print these sacks before use.

These sacks became the material for a new dress or new shirt for school. Mother taught Betty to do her own and she won prizes at 4-H club shows for her work. She was a senior in High School before she had a store bought dress.

Betty came in the nick of time. After five years another little girl graced our home and then there was another boy and another. The three were tagalongs that needed lots of nurturing. Betty accepted the role as second mother to the three tagalongs. She became the ruler of the kitchen.

Betty did everything with enthusiastic zeal. House flies were always a problem and she devised a way to diminish them. She left some melon rinds outside the kitchen door until a large contingent of flies congregated for a feast. She grabbed the broom and swiftly moved out the door and brought the broom down with a thud on the hapless creatures. The Broom handle broke but there were dead flies And melon mess in a wide circle around where the rinds had been.

Betty was barely in her teens when Pearl Harbor bombing occurred which suddenly took her older brothers. Father was used to having lots of hands in the field. Betty not only ran the kitchen but was used in pitching hay and milking cows and chores around the farm. As the war progressed many products were scarce. Betty canned 300 quarts of food one summer.

As a 4-H Club girl she won many prizes. She was on the girl's meat judging team for Alfalfa County that won first place at the state fair. She also showed farm animals at the fairs. She experienced a serious accident while trimming a lamb for the stock show. The lamb turned suddenly which threw the sharp point of the shears into her throat. barely missing the jugular.

She was elected basketball queen her senior year. She finished salutatorian of her high school graduating class. She was an outstanding leader of anything she put her mind to do.

The war was still on the year Betty graduated from High School. Some of her girl friends wanted to go into nurses training. That very month she came down with dangerous undulant fever. This eliminated her opportunity to take nurse training with her friends. A month later, after her friends were gone and the opportunity ceased. She was miraculously healed of her affliction.

She had been quite young at the time of the revival at Liberty church that brought such change to the family. In her young heart she decided to follow Jesus as her savior and had maintained a good relationship with God all through high school.

She went to Central College in Kansas and then to Greenville, Illinois College. She pursued a teacher's career. She taught Home Economics and English at Byers, Kansas one year. At her next assignment in

Partridge high school she met Donald Murray who ran the lumberyard in town. They were married.

Nine years later while teaching at Hutchinson Christian School a beautiful daughter was born. She named her Kelly. A Year later Donald Murray passed away

The young widow taught for another year in Hutchinson, then moved to Glencoe, Oklahoma where mother and father were retired. She built a house next door. She became a vital support to them in old age.

Needing a job, she started the Senior Center in Glencoe that was a great success.

Her biggest challenge came a few years later when she became program director and counselor at the Home of Redeeming Love in Oklahoma City. This position became an open door of a vast service to unwed mothers. She became Asst. Director in two years and then superintendent of the home later.

Betty had been a widow for eight years when she met and married Ralph Hollingshead, a kind, considerate complement to her "take charge" nature. The many years of marriage has shown what a blessing Ralph has been to Betty. The rest of the tribe of Jesse have experienced the warmth and hospitality of their home.

Betty has given vast service to others. I mentioned that she was born in the nick of time. It's quite apparent that she was born in the fullness of time to fill her service in a large family that prepared her for a larger service to many people. Like her two sisters she is also listed in WHO'S WHO OF AMERICAN WOMEN.

That's my sister; **"Lady Betty."**

The Three Who Came Late

It was like showing up for a baseball team when the nine players were already selected.. Was it like running for a prize that had been claimed nine times ahead of you?   It was like being called to a banquet and getting there late; Or coming off the road late at night and finding NO VACANCY signs, like Joseph & Mary on that Christmas eve long ago.

The situations stated above seemed to never enter the minds of the three children born in the depression. They were the play things of older siblings who enjoyed them and I think they enjoyed being there.

Mother had given away the iron bed with the white lead paint all chewed off. The nursery apparently was out of business for five years. Life had enough struggles already with three years of the great depression.

In the middle of the dust storms and droughts; Whoops, Lida Elaine number ten in the tribe of Jesse came along.

Ruthalie got married the same year so there was that space filled immediately. To my ten year old mind Lida was the most beautiful child I had ever seen. You couldn't buy a doll or toy at the most expensive store that was as real and fun loving as this one.

Lida had an intense curiosity She was barely able to walk before she knew how to climb up to reach the unreachable child proof areas. I remember that I was supposed to be watching over her one day.   Mother kept on a high shelf in the pantry some Walko tablets that were used in chicken's drinking water.   These things were chocolate color.

When Lida came out of the pantry with chocolate looking stuff drooling from her chin, I rushed to the pantry to see what she had found good to eat. There was the Walko tablet bottle with the cap off and all the tablets gone. I was horrified. Mother had gone to town and no one else was there to relieve my mind. When mother showed up I hurried to tell her about my little sister eating all the Walko tablets.

I suppose mother had seen it all and weathered through so many children's traumas that she appeared to be calm as she checked on the child. Anyway Lida Elaine was none the worse for it.   I think! The tablets are not poison or else it qualified under the scripture "if you drink any deadly thing, it will not hurt you."

Her idyllic childhood was cut short at the birth of a brother two years later. I remember the morning after as our neighbor lady, Lina Unruh, made the breakfast for the family. Father came in from the chores and announced: "I've had quite a night. The old sow had nine pigs, my best milk cow had a calf, and I got a new boy all the same night."

The depression had not lessened and the dusty desert was even more threatening when Vernon Samuel was born in the family. Father went up to Grandpa and Grandma Wayman's house to tell them about his boy born so near grandpa's birthday so they named him Sam. Grandma said, "I wouldn't even name my dog Sam."

The grandparents had so many grand children, what's another one? After a brief visit grandpa smiled through his mustache and said, "*By-dad*, Jesse, here's a half-dollar fer that new boy." The boy was a Wayman, with his tow-head and blue eyes and looked like his father.

The bed situation was more complicated for the three tag alongs. Sam tells how he usually got sleepy early and went upstairs to bed. In the morning he found himself on the floor. He thought he had fallen out of bed each night. He wondered how he managed to have a blanket around him on the floor, but never saw reason to ask.

The boy made it tough on Lida and Betty. His mind was keen on mischief and excelled among his peers as a humorist.. He put things to rhyme to tell his story and could make a mundane situation into a mammoth occasion with his witticisms. He was both fun and exasperating to have around as a kid.

I left home in 1942 with the Army and missed much of the lives of the three who came late. Sam had barely lost his baby teeth at that time and most of the years after were hearsay or brief intervals of family reunions.

When Sam lost his baby teeth and the new ones had not yet filled up the space; he delighted in tormenting his sisters by pulling a fishing worm out of his mouth through the space in his teeth. Since this was not polite behavior for the family, that was like 'sic' em' to a hound dog' for Sam. Mother just prayed harder, and father hitched up his team and drove off to the east place.

The caboose finally arrived almost two years after Vernon Samuel. The depression had only deepened as year after year the hopes of a bigger crop and a better price were not realized. 1936 opened with a dry winter and spring rains were not coming on time.. We children were up to the Unruh place for the day while Mrs. Unruh helped mother at the ranch house. We came home to another boy. He was fully exercising his lungs as if he knew that things were bad here and he was reluctant to join it.

Some have said that the youngest of big families are not bright. Our little brother certainly blew that theory. We got to help with the naming of this boy, Roger Jay. Or is it Jolly Roger, because he was a jolly little fellow? He loved attention and relished having no pen or crib to confine him. He was our toy that we liked a lot. The whole ranch was the play area of the three youngest and the family of older brothers and sisters enjoyed them all. Jay had a unique spot that none of the others had. He could be the baby of the family all his life. I think he enjoyed every bit of it. Who would want to be old enough to work when you could be too young to do much?

He was a husky built lad and we called him **One Ton Lug**. He didn't care what you called him as long as you called him for dinner. Sam & Jay, as different as brothers can be. By circumstances of birth were thrown together as cohorts in mischief, sibling in rivalry, and bonded as brothers.

Ruthalie's first son was born about eight months after Sam. His name was James Terrell Heffner. In another eight months Roger Jay was born an uncle. One summer Ruthalie visited the ranch with her son James T. Sam and Jay were involved with him in constant play around the farm yard. The boys played well together.

Mother raised hybrid chickens. The eggs were sold for a little extra at a hatchery in Enid. The manager of the hatchery, Ms. Blaylock, came out to cull the chickens one day. She noticed the three tow-heads running around the yard and of course the older children coming and going all day. She finally asked sister Betty. "Are two of those boys twins by chance?" Betty replied like a eleven year old, "Oh no, they are eight months apart." No further explanation was given. The poor lady had to quench her curiosity with the obvious. "No wonder the Wayman's have so many children; they're only eight months apart."

Jay was built more for power. He exuded self confidence. In sibling rivalry with Sam, Jay got so he could whip his older brother. Jay showed stock and won many prizes in 4-H club. He was mechanical minded in that he could work on machinery and liked to make things that revealed his talents for his life's work.

Sam was built for speed but didn't recognize it as a talent. When Jay whipped him, it was a major put down.. This was frustrating for an older brother. Sam never resigned himself to being on the bottom. He fought with a boy at school as I myself did years before. When I found myself on the bottom of the heap, I calculated I was built for speed and never sought another role. But Sam tantalized the Sedbrook boy and was whipped over and over. The recess bell saved him each time. He was a determined boy to excel no matter if he had little ability for it.

Sam tells about some of his escapes from tragedy while on the farm. He was running the tractor on the plow into the evening as the custom was in harvest. The tractor would be needed for the combine in the day. He needed to refill the tractor with gas at the trap-wagon. It was nearly dark. He was pumping gas into a ten gal can. He could not see how full the can was. Without thinking, he struck a match. The gas vapor on a hot night immediately engulfed him and the wagon in flames. He had the presence of mind to quickly place the lid on the can, which extinguished the flames. Outside of burned hair and face he was wiser for his mistake.

Another time he took the new pick up to go to brothers house a half mile away to get something. It was a hot day and no air conditioning in those days. The windows were opened and a hornet managed to get in and buzz around his head. Sam took his eye off the road and his hat off his head to drive the hornet out of the cab. The pickup left the road and hit the only electric pole in the area. The damage to the new pick up was severe.

Sam drove back home heartsick. He went upstairs to bed thinking father would thresh him for this. He heard the stair well door open and heard his fathers steps come up the stairway. He dared not look for fear of what he thought was his just dessert. Father sat on his bed and said, "Sam, I know you feel badly for wrecking the pick-up, but I remember how I wrecked both of my Model T's when I was a younger man." Sam thought a lot more of his dad after that and in fact as I hear the story from Sam, my opinion of my father is much enriched.

Lida graduated at the head of her high school class at Goltry High School. She was able to go that fall to Central College in Kansas and then out to Seattle Pacific Univ. She was hired as a teacher at the town of Sequim in Washington state. She may have been there yet except a class mate from Goltry kept writing to her.

Gene Cooper was more than a class mate. His father had been pastor at our country church when the younger of the Wayman tribe came along. Rev Cooper was a down to earth country preacher that the farmers all liked. He was hired by the farmers to work for them to supplement the meager salary of the waning congregation. Even my father thought Rev. Cooper was his kind of preacher, because he was not afraid of hard work.

Pastor Cooper had one son , Gene, who was in Lida's class at school. He also saw her every Sunday at the Liberty Church They were fun friends at home. When Gene joined the army and Lida went to college they found occasion to pursue a course that led to marriage. From there Lida traveled wherever her army career husband went, to Germany to Thailand and near army bases in the US. Lida took more schooling and became a very successful business lady as a CPA. She headed up an accounting business in San Antonio many years

Lida is listed in WHO'S WHO of AMERICAN WOMEN.

She is such a gracious lady. She can entertain the whole family reunion and do it like its fun. Yes, I think I'm pretty smart to raise such a fine sister.

Sam finished high school at Goltry. At Liberty Church he made a commitment of his life to Christ. Four of the older brothers had answered the Call of God to the ministry. One day Sam told mother that he was called to preach and wanted to go to the Cumberland Presbyterian College in McKenzie, Tennessee. Mother had calculated that Sam did not have a serious bone in his body. She told us later that she was surprised when Sam heard the call of God on his life and entered the ministry. Come to think of it, she said the same thing when I told her about my call ten years earlier. You can't tell how high the eagle can fly unless you turn him loose.

Sam has pastored many churches He is the only one still with the Cumberland Presbyterian movement. This is the group that LIBERTY Church was affiliated with. Sam is the only one who has attained a Doctorate. Father always made fun of the People who wore the Square Cap. All the family but Dean did that very thing.

The folks bought a place to retire in Glencoe and then two more farms to go with it there. It was part of fathers plan to furnish a farm for any of the boys who would stay. Jay was only a Junior in High school when this happened. He opted to stay with bachelor brother, Clarence, up on the home place and finish his high school at Goltry. Jay showed hogs with great success but paid enough attention to his study to graduate from Goltry High School in 1954.

He was the benefactor of a new record for the Goltry High School. Mother and Father went back up for the graduation. When Jay was to get his diploma, the Superintendent. called mother up to make the presentation. ALL TWELVE CHILDREN HAD GRADUATED FROM THE GOLTRY HIGH SCHOOL IN A TWENTY-TWO YEAR PERIOD. Mother handed Jay his diploma and kissed him. No one else could come close to that record, but I suppose no one else cares to.

Jay started at Stillwater A&M College but went right away into the army. He was stationed at Ft Leonard Wood Missouri. He and a buddy went to a roller skating rink. The events seem a little murky but somehow he was clumsy and fell into a lovely young lady named Pauline.

After the embarrassment of the moment the apologies led to a shaky romance. Jay happened to be writing to two girls at the same time and managed the clumsy act of mixing up the envelopes. The next meeting with Pauline was cold as Siberia until he discovered his mishap. He had to explain his way out of the awkward situation. Fortunately he had found a very understanding young lady and they married right away, lest he blunder again. He had barely turned twenty.

After graduating from college he became college professor at Corpus Christi Texas, teaching mechanics to kids who had no talent for office jobs.

While teaching he had a boat that he took his family out in the gulf waters. One day he got caught in the propeller that severed an artery. This event nearly cost him his life.

Jay made a new commitment to God and serves as an elder in his Methodist church.. His fascination in the rest of the family that grew up before him has caused hours of research and work. He restored the **Model T without a Top** and the old horse drawn buggy.

The famous buggy had served the folks before marriage. It had also served the older children through Fairview School. It was retired from active duty when the family moved over the hill to the west place. The shafts were gone and it was a family plaything. The younger three had no emotional attachment to the old transportation.

One day after Sunday church, Sam, Jay and the Lingo boy of their age went with Lida for a ride in the old buggy like we had done years before. It had no shafts to guide; only a rope reins to pull the way you wanted to turn. They pushed it up the hill on the east place and then all got on to ride down the hill. The steering method was not good. The buggy gained speed but headed for the deep canyon. The riders all bailed off to save their lives. The buggy crashed to its grave in the deep canyon.

The remains of it were there many years until Jay confessed to the crime and named his accomplices. He resurrected the buggy piece by piece and put it together again.

He made a complete model of the farm yard with the house and buildings on the farm where he was born. He also, from pictures, restored a model of the east place farm house where the first nine children were born. He is a mechanical genius. I don't guess he came late. God held him up until he could fit in a place no one else could fill as well as he did. Omega!

Liberty Church

The narrative of the Cherokee Strip early days would not be complete without a mention of the profound influence of the church. The country schools were built by the early settlers to accommodate large families. The churches were considered as important as the schools.

Fairview School doubled as a community church. Then in 1907 a one eyed preacher by the name of McCord led the people to build their own church. McCord was of pioneer stock himself. He preached with a group of Presbyterian folk who had experienced great revivals a century earlier in the Cumberland country. They called themselves Cumberland Presbyterians. They tended to follow the way west, opening new churches.

These were rugged men of the cloth who came with the settlers to new areas. They sacrificed greatly and worked with their hands to build a church for the Glory of God and the instruction of the people. All the simple buildings were from donated labor and materials. The whole community would cooperate more or less together. It was the neighborly thing to do.

The early settlers found their fraternization at the school and the church. Itinerant preachers would come and hold protracted meeting that would always attract good crowds. There was no time nor place for amusements, so preachin' was valued highly.

Black was black, and white was white, at the meeting house. You knew that the preaching was good when the worst sinner in the neighborhood '**got Religion**'. Many wrongs were made right and confessions came forth of all the deviltry that had gone on before. Even the non-religious were benefited by the better behavior of neighbors who were affected by the strong preaching. Restitution was a common occurrence among the converted.

LIBERTY was the church of choice for many within horse and buggy driving distance. Up to the beginning of the depression days, the church had reached to a full house status on preaching Sunday.

The exodus of farmers during the depression was devastating for the country church. Farms were foreclosed and some dusted out in the droughts. The Pastors had no place to live or anything to live on. Town churches called them away and by early thirties the last young minister and wife left.

There were a few of the faithful folk who remained. They all had families so they still came on Sunday morning for Sunday School. Mother taught the adult class. Other adults changed off teaching the various age levels of children. The Tarrant families, the Wells, the Tarrs, the Lingos, the Yorks, the Blues, the Castors, the Pattons, and a few others kept the church alive for many years. Mother and the girls kept the Waymans represented. The boys went only occasionally. Father did not go too much and we boys were going less and less. It looked like LIBERTY was done for and many folks didn't care.

Mother was used to battling difficulties. She was reared in a devout family. To see her own children slipping carelessly was a deep concern. She would gather us around after breakfast at the ranch and read a scripture and pray hard for Jesse and the children every day. She was a good story teller and she made Bible stories interesting. Her prayers were pertinent to the need of the day. She prayed for rain in the dust and drought. She thanked God when we got a little and pled for more. She asked God to watch over her family and keep us from the snares and pitfalls. That was part of the prayer that I felt the keenest. Her prayers were piling up. God works in strange ways His wonders to perform.

I loved 4-H Club. The year I bought the purebred Poland China sow I was into the fitting and showing life. I was fourteen when my fat pig won first prize at the county fair. The county agent wanted us to send the pig to the state fair with the load going from the county. We put the pig on the truck and I rode with the county agent to Oklahoma City. I had never been that far away from home so long. Father gave me four dollars to live on for five days at the fair.

I laid my sleeping bag down in the aisle of the hog barn and slept the first night. The next day I wandered up under the bright lights of the side shows. My eye bugged out and my mouth agape at the unusual sights I saw. Some sneak slipped my billfold out of my pocket while I was looking on.

I had only a nickel in my pocket. I had four days yet to go. I could see myself starving to death by then. I didn't know what to do; to beg I was ashamed. I was afraid to tell anyone because I didn't want them to think I was incapable of taking care of myself. The only food I had was the grain for the pig and I fain would have filled my belly with what he ate.

That night I could not sleep. I crawled out of my sleeping bag and walked out away from the barn. I lifted my face toward heaven and prayed the first heart-felt prayer in my life. "God I don't know if you know who I am, I'm one of Jesse Wayman's boys. I've lost my money and I do not know what to do. If you could help me, I surely would appreciate it." "What's That? a Tear!" It's not the code to cry. I went back inside to bed.

The next morning I showed my pig in the ring. The ring was crowded with sixty-five pigs in the class. I barely won anything. A neighbor man that I knew was there that morning. He said to me, "Why don't you let one of the other boys take care of the pig the rest of the week and I'll take you home this evening."

I was delivered at my home that evening. I had starved to death for twenty four hours. I was awed by this experience. Think of it, a God in Heaven knew who I was. My father even could never get the kids straight and he was with us every day. He often called me "Dean James Clarence Byron Phil" when he spoke to me.

God knew who I was the first time I asked him for anything. This was in my mind the greatest miracle in my life. I know, its no biggie to you, but it was for me. I started back to Sunday School the next Sunday to find out more about a God who cares about me. **Even me!**

Laveta Wells was my teacher in the high school class at Liberty. She cared about what her students were doing. She made a big deal out of the fact that I won first prize at the County Fair. You can feel lost in a big family. Laveta seemed to sense that I needed a little bit of approval. I listened in class.

All the Wayman children younger than I attended Sunday School from then on without trying to sneak out of it. Other teen-agers began to attend the class also. LaVeta Wells talked about being *saved.* I didn't know what that meant and none of my friends talked about getting it. I'd heard about some going to heaven and some not. I certainly wanted to go to heaven when I died. The other option was a place to avoid at all costs. I was in no hurry to go either place right away.

I could not see faults in other people because I became conscious that I was the worst sinner in the world. After Sunday School one day the following summer I went across the hill to the old homestead house. I threw myself across a bed and cried out to God, "Oh God, send us a preacher, so I can get 'Saved'.

That very fall a small pox epidemic broke out in the town of Nash. The pastor of the Baptist church found his church on quarantine along with the schools for awhile. He remembered seeing the Liberty Church way out there in the country. He inquired and found that there was a Sunday School there but no preaching service. He found one of the stalwarts of the church and asked about coming to hold a protracted meeting while his church was quarantined. Would they like it? "Yes! Yes! Yes!"

When the announcement was made on Sunday morning about the preacher coming that night, I knew it, 'that's God's answer to my Prayer'.

Mother was always faithful to meetings. I planned to go and all the younger ones in the family did the same. In my heart I had mixed emotions. Maybe no one will come so I can get saved without anyone noticing. Maybe the preacher won't make an appeal to young people. I hoped none of my peers would be there. I hoped my father wouldn't go, but he did.

The house was full for the first night. I found my security among the big boys on the back row. A young lady from the Baptist Church in Nash led the singing. The preacher took his text. **"The Son of Man has come to seek and to save that which is lost."**

It seemed like someone had told the preacher about me. I knew I fit every thing he said about being "Lost". He came to the end. Like a good Baptist, he gave the invitation to accept Christ. I debated with myself, "What will my friends think? I'll wait for a night when there are less people: My Dad won't like it. I'm in the middle of the pew and these big boys will hold me back."

God was stronger than all my excuses. I had pled for a preacher, and here he is, and he is inviting me, now GO!. I started toward the aisle, the big boys between me and the aisle melted like wax in a hot flame. I am not accountable for others, I am only accountable to God for what happened. It worked for me. I had found **Peace** and I determined to never look back.

The change in the family was gradual. Robert made his commitment in the same revival. Hugh and Betty both were greatly affected by it. Byron came in later. James and Clarence made commitments in different churches. Dean became an Elder in the Church at Liberty after WWII. Lida, Sam and Jay were greatly influenced by the church. Many other young people of the community were greatly guided and helped by the teaching of the country church that was almost dead.

The Call

A minister, Rev Bolding came to Liberty to revival meeting. A young lady, Opal Combs, came and led the singing. She was a great blessing to our family. Byron found Peace with God that established his life after his broiler business burned. I prayed my first public prayer at that time. It was springtime and I was cultivating the corn. I was singing some of the choruses that Opal Combs was teaching us. All of a sudden I experienced such Joy that my heart overflowed with the love of God.

The Liberty church took on new life. Many of the families had experienced some affects of the revival. There was a sister church thirty miles away at Amorita. They wanted to hire a pastor but depression had lessened their attendance. They agreed to share a Pastor every other week with us at Liberty. Rev Newton came to us. A good man with teen-agers himself. He preached every other week. He led us in painting and fixing up the building and brought in electricity.

I graduated from high school in the spring. I became full-time hand on the farm. Father paid nothing to start with, but doubled the wages every month. His fleeting dream of Empire required all of us working desperately until he could give us our own farm. I worked the harvest and the threshing crew.

I was plowing after the early rain on the Constant farm that we rented. I liked to plow with the Case tractor turning over four furrows at once. I was singing above the noise of the tractor enjoying the day. As I studied the stubble being turned over, it seemed like that's the way life was with me. I was turning under the trash of my life and the clean smell of fresh soil was being exposed for something new.

When I tell what happened next, I am very aware of misunderstandings. No two persons have the exact same experiences. God deals with us individually. There is no way I can prove it, but it is as real to me today as it was many years ago. I'm telling it the way it was.

Above the roar of the tractor a still small voice said, "I want you to preach the gospel!" " **No**," I responded. I felt betrayed. In my mind, I envisioned the poor pastor from the church coming down to visit the ranch. His car was misfiring and his clothes were patched; the picture of poverty. I'd seen that kind of life already. I could not deny the reality of **the Call.** I had found abundant life and longed for more. I finally said "Yes" to God. I answered **the Call** but what do I do now?

I needed some confirmation of **the Call** lest I had heard in vain. Reverend Newton, the following

Sunday preached on "How to know you are Called of God." It spoke to me clearly. As I was going out the door after church, the pastor put his big hand in mine and said, "Phil, isn't God calling you to ministry?"

How to tell the family was a problem. I finally told Mother. She was surprised. I wanted to go that fall to college to study for the ministry. Father reacted as I expected, negatively. In his mind the only reason anyone would want to go preach was because he was too lazy to work. He said emphatically, "I need the boys to help with the work."

I was in a turmoil in my heart. I wanted to follow God and yet I was forbidden to do so. I'm only eighteen. I had in mind to pack my suitcase, run away to a college town and work my way through. It was obvious that father could not afford sending me. Now he'd made it clear that he did not want me in the ministry.

I went one night into the garden and lifted my face to God. I told God that I didn't think it was fair, for Him to call me to do something that I didn't want to do, and then close the door on me so that I couldn't do it. A scripture came into my mind. **Honor your father and your mother that your days may be long upon the Earth.** It was easy to honor mother, she was in shock, but favorable. To honor father was the supreme test of my life. God gave me His grace to honor and obey my father, for how long I did not know.

The folks at Liberty wanted me to start preaching every other week that Rev. Newton could not come. I learned a lot about failure. The grace of the people was so apparent to put up with me. I don't understand people saying, "there are too many hypocrites in the church." After Liberty experience I have a profound respect for the old fashioned folks who nurtured us in difficult times. It's the hardest place in the world to preach to people whom you respect as solid citizens of the kingdom. They had taught me all I knew.

My break came with the dastardly deed of Dec 7, 1941. Three of the older brothers went into the Navy. The draft age was lowered from twenty-one to eighteen. I turned twenty and Hugh turned eighteen the following spring. I was put in I-A immediately.

It was nearly harvest time when my father said to me, "Phil, lets go see the Draft Board" I didn't know what he wanted to tell them. We put on our best overalls, our farm work shoes, and straw hats and drove to Cherokee to meet with the draft board. It was at the courthouse where I had been many times in my 4-H club work. Our hard soled shoes clanged loudly on the marble floors.

We entered a court room where three judges sat at a table. Fumbling with our straw hats we approached the bench. Father spoke up. "My son, Phil, has a call into the ministry and you've got him in 1-A". I couldn't believe my ears what my father was admitting. The long solemn faces of the three judges showed no emotion. One spoke to me:

"Young man, are you licensed or ordained for Ministry?" I replied, "No, Sir."

"Are you in College or Seminary studying for the Ministry?" "No Sir."

"Then are you preaching in a church?" "No Sir."

"Then what are you doing?" "I'm helping pop on the farm.

"Hiding a smirk", he said, "Well, we can't let every Tom, Dick and Harry out, just because they all of a sudden have a call to preach."

The interview was over quickly and we walked out. Can you imagine the belly laugh those men enjoyed after we were out of hearing. We drove home in silence. I did not care what happened, I had honored my father, only to have it turn to another hurdle before I could follow the Call. With me my father never expressed opposition again. His spirit was broken, but he could not bring himself to apologize.

As I look back on that event from the fulfillment of a long life I've enjoyed, I can see the hand of God in it all. I had the privilege of helping father to pray a prayer of faith in Christ in later years. I went through dangers of war including two Philippine beach heads. I suffered Heart fibrillation at forty-two. Insurance companies refused to insure me after that. I have led the Royal Ranger program for boys. I have hiked the crest trail in full pack many years. I have been abroad nine times. I have pioneered and built churches and my own homes. I have had a full life of gospel ministry for fifty years.

I have enjoyed what God promised in the garden behind the ranch house. **Honor your father and your Mother that your days may be long on the earth.**

To tell the full story of what happened after becoming a soldier in the US Army would be another book. I did not intend to tell my story, but rather the one that my mother started over a hundred years ago. I wanted to show how we had the best of two worlds. We had a father who taught us how to work and a mother who taught us how to pray. Church life had such profound effect on the family.

We were the generation of vast social upheaval in America but we were the ones who stuck it out. Crying fixes no fence but hard work and prayer will build strong character.

Five of the nine Wayman boys became ministers. We have all built churches. We have worked in Pioneer situations where there was nothing or little to start with like our parents and grandparents before us.

Addenda::   It is worthy of note that the Pioneer James Secord was a teacher & farmer.   His children were college professors,. school teachers, ministers and farmers.   Mildred's twelve children became college professors, school teachers, ministers and farmers.

The story of the Secord family whose faith and confidence in God never wavered through extreme times, is still being lived through their children and children's children. This is not only true of Mildred whose story I am honored to tell, but also of the other Arrows *in Grandfathers Quiver*. * They are blessed to the third and fourth generation. We who were fortunate enough to be beneficiaries have inherited more than the land empire that my father envisioned.

Revisit Ps. 127:4,5

The Way It Was

(Family gathering when boys all came home from war)
Back row l. to r.: James, Robert, Byron, Dean, Hugh
Middle row: l.to r.: Sam, Phil, Clarence, Jay
Front row: l to r: Betty, Lida, Jesse, Mildred, Ruthalie

The Way it Was

It surely was not purely chance
that brought such transition to the ranch.
Depression days with dust and drought
kept us hustling all about.
Just to keep the family fed
while debts piled higher in the red.
Father stewed and mother prayed;
kids grew and house shrank where we stayed.

We'd have joined the Grapes of wrath
but debts were too much to follow that path.
Harvest time and what did we get
another mouth to feed and deeper in debt.

Until the minus worth exceeded
the total value of what we needed.
The only hope for all the toil
was someday we would strike some oil.

The big men came with long black cars,
they dickered and puffed on big cigars.
The piddly lease money would pay the tax
and keep us from falling under the ax.

It was Sunday December 7th of forty one,
at Pearl Harbor a deadly bombing run.
It might as well have dropped on the Ranch
as they were taking a risky chance.

The boys all experts with the rifle
responded to teach them not to trifle
First one then several others
until there was a total of five brothers.
Fighting a people they could not see
out of patriotism for our country.

With Uncle Sam taking boys out of reach
God called some more to preach.
Dreams of a farming empire shattered
like exploding bombs the boys all scattered.

Girls married, moved away
with nothing left but debts to pay.
The short handed ranch was still there and yet
so also was the mammoth debt..

The toil the plans, the life the farmer gave
was buried with him in the grave.
But death does not stop the generation
that sprang to life like a new creation.

From two to twelve there are now alive
considerably more that fifty five.
The house and barn decay with rot
but in Eternity your children are all you've got.

Sam Wayman
Tribe of Jesse #10

The Stock Tank Behind the Shed

Twas a might important fixture out on the ranch.
Neath a mulberry tree the livestock had a chance
To endure days of summer with sun bearing down.
Ponds and creeks went dry for many miles around.
At the stock tank the cattle gathered in the shade.
To drink their fill and dawdle in the shadow it made.

There was competition on a red hot summer day,
For boys sweating hard and dusty from pitching hay.
'Twas plumb refreshing to sneak a little prank,
And do some skinny dippin' in the old stock tank.
Papa warned us to not pollute it, rilin' up the water.
Cause the cattle had to drink it as the day got hotter.

We'd sneak down after dark when time to go to bed,
and take a little plunge in the tank behind the shed.
Mama didn't like to have sheets all muddied up,
as if boys were fighting with full coffee cups.
But without shoes or clothes or making any noise,
We'd sneak some skinny dippin' with just us boys.

One eve we were swimmin' our clothes back in bed,
When neighbors came to visit.& parked by the shed.
They talked and talked like country folk like to do,
With us laying low in water, and getting colder too.
We crept across the corral, the field and garden place,
Arriving at the back porch, muddy from foot to face.
We sighed with relief, in the dark we slipped in bed
Messing up everything because of the tank behind
the shed.

Now that I'm sophisticated, I have a big white tub,
The hot water is expensive each time I take a scrub.
The washer often leaks, or the tub needs cleaning out
They even charge for the water coming out the spout.
It costs a fortune to install tho its not one whit better.
Than the old stock tank, and certainly its no wetter.
They tax me a lot higher, for any tub they've seen,
and add lots more to it if I keep it looking clean.

For the Sheer Joy of Living when it time to go to bed.
I prefer Skinny Dippin' in the tank behind the shed.

The Forsaken Farmhouse

I saw a house on an old homestead
Its space was hollow and bare.
the doors were sagging and broken glass
was strewn abound everywhere.

The garden gate rusts and fences droop,
weeds stand ragged and tall.
The floor joists sadly bend with rot
Inside the tottering wall.

The roof line sags in mourning deep
Its windows blindly stare
At the world that might have been
If people were still living there.

I fancied a time when the house was home
to a family happy and free
Who hallowed the place with laughter and song
Though humble their dwelling be.

I envisioned a man and woman there
laboring in honest toil.
I heard the voices of children at play
roaming its acres of soil.

The place was alive, the house a home
Hewed out of the prairie sod.
When its homey rafters rang
With singing and prayers to God.

A family who loved her and called her home
is like a husband in the prime of life.
Doting on his lady fair,
The best in married life.

Now she's forsaken her dreams are crushed
Like a husband who has gone away.
And abandoned her to live alone
With only memories of yesterday.

The empty house, like a forsaken wife
sits forlornly alone
Waiting for time to bring hope again.
and restore the house to a home.

Phil Wayman # 6 tribe of Jesse

to R: Bob. Jay, Byron, Sam, Phil, Clarence, Dean, Lida
L to R: James, Betty, Father, Mother, Ruthalie, Hugh - 1958

ISBN 141200431-4

9 781412 004312